"Is this your room or mine?"
Lindsay asked Gil.

Dead silence. He didn't even look at her.

"Gil? Is this—"

"Our room."

It was her turn to be silent.

His gaze met hers. "There was only one room left. We can't go on, and we can't stay in the car. I didn't know what to do but take the room. I promise you you're in no danger from me."

She believed him. And she should've been grateful. She *was* grateful, she hurriedly assured herself. But he needn't make it sound so easy.

All afternoon, closed up in her small car, his male aura had kept her aware, tense…interested, no matter how much she told herself she wasn't attracted to him.

Now she was goi~~~
with him?

Dear Reader,

As Silhouette's yearlong anniversary celebration continues, Romance again delivers six unique stories about the poignant journey from courtship to commitment.

Teresa Southwick invites you back to STORKVILLE, USA, where a wealthy playboy has the gossips stumped with his latest transaction: *The Acquired Bride*...and her triplet kids! *New York Times* bestselling author Kasey Michaels contributes the second title in THE CHANDLERS REQUEST... miniseries, *Jessie's Expecting*. Judy Christenberry spins off her popular THE CIRCLE K SISTERS with a story involving a blizzard, a roadside motel with one bed left, a gorgeous, honor-bound rancher...and his *Snowbound Sweetheart*.

New from Donna Clayton is SINGLE DOCTOR DADS! In the premiere story of this wonderful series, a first-time father strikes *The Nanny Proposal* with a woman whose timely hiring quickly proves less serendipitous and more carefully, *lovingly*, staged.... Lilian Darcy pens yet another edgy, uplifting story with *Raising Baby Jane*. And debut author Jackie Braun delivers pure romantic fantasy as a down-on-her-luck waitress receives an intriguing order from the man of her dreams: *One Fiancée To Go, Please*.

Next month, look for the exciting finales of STORKVILLE, USA and THE CHANDLERS REQUEST... And the wait is over as Carolyn Zane's BRUBAKER BRIDES make their grand reappearance!

Happy Reading!

Mary-Theresa Hussey

Mary-Theresa Hussey
Senior Editor

Please address questions and book requests to:
Silhouette Reader Service
U.S.: 3010 Walden Ave., P.O. Box 1325, Buffalo, NY 14269
Canadian: P.O. Box 609, Fort Erie, Ont. L2A 5X3

Snowbound
Sweetheart

JUDY CHRISTENBERRY

SILHOUETTE *Romance*®
Published by Silhouette Books
America's Publisher of Contemporary Romance

For Finis Christenberry, a good man through and through

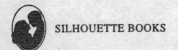 SILHOUETTE BOOKS

ISBN 0-373-19476-5

SNOWBOUND SWEETHEART

Copyright © 2000 by Judy Christenberry

Printed in U.S.A.

Books by Judy Christenberry

Silhouette Romance

The Nine-Month Bride #1324
*Marry Me, Kate #1344
*Baby in Her Arms #1350
*A Ring for Cinderella #1356
†Never Let You Go #1453
†The Borrowed Groom #1457
†Cherish the Boss #1463
†Snowbound Sweetheart #1476

*Lucky Charm Sisters
†The Circle K Sisters

JUDY CHRISTENBERRY

has been writing romances for over fifteen years because she loves happy endings as much as her readers do. She's a bestselling writer for Harlequin American Romance, but she has a long love of traditional romances and is delighted to tell a story that brings those elements to the reader. A former high school French teacher, Judy devotes her time to writing. She hopes readers have as much fun reading her stories as she does writing them. She spends her spare time reading, watching her favorite sports teams and keeping track of her two adult daughters.

IT'S OUR 20ᵗʰ ANNIVERSARY!
We'll be celebrating all year,
Continuing with these fabulous titles,
On sale in October 2000.

Desire

#1321 The Dakota Man
Joan Hohl

#1322 Rancher's Proposition
Anne Marie Winston

#1323 First Comes Love
Elizabeth Bevarly

#1324 Fortune's Secret Child
Shawna Delacorte

#1325 Marooned With a Marine
Maureen Child

#1326 Baby: MacAllister-Made
Joan Elliott Pickart

Romance

#1474 The Acquired Bride
Teresa Southwick

#1475 Jessie's Expecting
Kasey Michaels

#1476 Snowbound Sweetheart
Judy Christenberry

#1477 The Nanny Proposal
Donna Clayton

#1478 Raising Baby Jane
Lilian Darcy

#1479 One Fiancée To Go, Please
Jackie Braun

Special Edition

#1351 Bachelor's Baby Promise
Barbara McMahon

#1352 Marrying a Delacourt
Sherryl Woods

#1353 Millionaire Takes a Bride
Pamela Toth

#1354 A Bundle of Miracles
Amy Frazier

#1355 Hidden in a Heartbeat
Patricia McLinn

#1356 Stranger in a Small Town
Ann Roth

Intimate Moments

#1033 Who Do You Love?
Maggie Shayne/
Marilyn Pappano

#1034 Her Secret Weapon
Beverly Barton

#1035 A Thanksgiving to Remember
Margaret Watson

#1036 The Return of Luke McGuire
Justine Davis

#1037 The Lawman Meets His Bride
Meagan McKinney

#1038 The Virgin Beauty
Claire King

Chapter One

Lindsay Crawford was going home. True, it was only for the Thanksgiving holiday, but she was looking forward to presenting the new Lindsay to her family. She made the rounds of her apartment, watering her plants one last time, so that her neighbor would only have to water them once while she was gone.

She set her bags out into the hall and pulled the door behind her, locking it. Then she crossed the hall to the opposite door, knocked and waited for Kathy to answer.

Instead of her friend, though, a tall, handsome man opened the door. The biggest surprise of all, however, was his attire. Instead of Chicago chic, or city casual, as most of the men Lindsay met in the city wore, he was dressed in worn jeans, a flannel shirt and boots. Just like her brothers back home.

"Uh, is Kathy here?"

"Yeah. Just a sec." He turned and called her neighbor's name over his shoulder. Then he opened the door wider. "Come on in."

Lindsay stepped inside the door just as Kathy came into the living area.

"Lindsay! You haven't left yet?"

"No, I thought I'd bring over my key. You said you wouldn't mind watering my plants. I just—"

"So your flight's still on?" Kathy interrupted.

Lindsay stared at her. "Why wouldn't it be?"

"Well, Gil's flight was canceled," Kathy replied. "Oh, I haven't introduced you. This is my brother, Gil Daniels. Gil, my neighbor Lindsay Crawford."

Lindsay nodded at the handsome man. "I suppose I should've checked on my flight, but the bad weather's not supposed to hit until tonight, so I didn't think there'd be a problem."

"That's what I thought, too," the man said, his voice deep and rich. "But the plane I'm on originated in Minneapolis. It's stuck there."

Lindsay could sympathize, but she figured he'd just catch the next one out. "Well, I hope you get out before the storm." She turned to Kathy. "Here's the key. And I just watered the plants, so probably watering them on Saturday will be enough."

"Aren't you going to call and check on your plane?" Kathy asked. "Maybe you and Gil were on the same flight."

Both she and Gil spoke at once. "I'm sure we're not."

Then they stared at each other.

"But aren't you from Oklahoma?" Kathy asked.

"Yes, but—" Lindsay stopped and stared at the man. "You were flying to Oklahoma?"

"Yeah, the three-thirty flight."

"Oh, no! No, that can't—well, I'll find another flight." She turned around to head for her apartment and the nearest phone.

"Won't do you any good," his laconic voice informed her.

She spun around to stare at him.

Kathy answered her unspoken question. "Gil's called every airline he could think of. They offered a flight tomorrow morning...if the storm hasn't closed the airport."

The weather forecasters were expecting a huge snowstorm this evening, but Lindsay hadn't really been concerned. After all, they were usually alarmists. And it was early for a snowstorm, even in Chicago.

The panic filling her had no basis. Missing Thanksgiving with her family wasn't the end of the world.

Except that she was homesick.

Extremely homesick.

She instantly formed a new plan. Nothing was going to stop her from getting home. She smiled at the other two. "Then I'll drive."

"I already checked. There aren't any rental cars available. I guess because of the holiday," Gil said, watching her.

Aha. She had him there. "I have my own car. I can load up and be out of here in half an hour, long before the storm hits Chicago." With a smile of triumph, she spun on her heel and was out in the hall when he called to her.

"Could I buy a seat in your car?"

Lindsay turned to stare at him. Her imagination immediately pictured the two of them enclosed in her tiny car, practically on top of each other. Heat pooled in her stomach. Which was ridiculous. He was Kathy's brother. The way her friend talked about him, he was a saint.

"Uh, my car is small."

"I could spell you on the driving."

That offer made her reconsider her decision. After all, she had at least fifteen hours of driving ahead of her. It was after one o'clock now. She'd need to drive straight through to get home by tomorrow morning.

Kathy spoke before Lindsay could, a disturbed look on her face. "Gil, I wish you'd stay. Brad and I would love to have you here for Thanksgiving."

"Sorry, baby, but I promised Rafe I'd be back tonight."

His calling his sister baby might have been thought endearing, but not to Lindsay. She'd grown up with five brothers and a father watching her every move, trying to direct every step. The phrase "baby" always grated on her nerves.

The man turned back to Lindsay. "I'll certainly be willing to pay all the expenses."

She gave him a long look. He was a stranger. But she'd known Kathy a year and really liked her. And Kathy adored her brother. That should be reference enough. Her family certainly wouldn't object. They'd probably approve of her having a man to "protect" her. How irritating!

Even so, she made her decision. "All right, Mr. Daniels. But I'm leaving in half an hour."

"I'm ready. Are you going dressed like that?"

She stiffened. Although she hadn't really thought about it, she probably would've changed.

Now she wouldn't do so for any amount of money.

Knee-jerk reaction, she knew. But she'd come all the way to Chicago to get away from men who thought they knew better than her.

"I don't think that's any of your business." She didn't wait for his response. She crossed the hall, unlocked her door, entered and slammed it behind her.

"Men!" she exclaimed under her breath. She could do without them.

"Oh, dear. I hope she doesn't go without you, Gil. I think you upset her."

"Good guess, baby," he said with a rueful grin. "City girls can be touchy, can't they?"

"But if she's from Oklahoma, she can't really be a city girl."

"Oklahoma City's bigger than you think, Kathy. They've even got some decent restaurants there. You'll have to come see me in the spring."

"Yes, of course, if Brad wants to."

Gil pressed his lips tightly together. He'd flown up because his sister had called yesterday crying. When he'd arrived this morning, she'd assured him she was just a little blue. Everything was fine.

He didn't believe her.

"Listen, Kathy, I want you to take this." He reached into his back pocket and pulled out his wallet. He took a plastic card from inside and gave it to her. "Put it away, and don't mention it to Brad. If you ever need money or...want to get away...for a visit or something, you can use it." Were his reasons tactful enough?

"Brad and I don't have secrets," Kathy assured him, looking at the card doubtfully, her hand creeping across her stomach.

"Are you all right?" he asked, watching her.

"Yes. Lately my stomach's been a little unsettled. But I'm just not sure about—"

"Just for once, do what I ask. It won't hurt anything to have a resource Brad doesn't know about. If you don't ever use it, it won't matter. But I'll feel better. Do it for me."

He breathed a sigh of relief when she finally took the charge card.

"Do you have a place to hide it?"

"I'll just put it in my billfold."

"No! No, let's find another place." He took her into her bedroom. "How about taped to the bottom of this mirror thing," he suggested, pointing to a mirror tray on her dresser.

"Okay."

She got some tape and did as he requested. Then he asked to borrow a couple of pillows and several blankets. "Just in case we run into bad weather. And maybe a jug of drinking water."

He hoped distracting her from what she'd just done would make her forget her objections.

Half an hour later, Lindsay rapped on Kathy's door again. Because she wasn't an idiot, she'd exchanged her heels for loafers. But she carried her heels with her, in a tote bag, so she could put them on before she got out of the car when she got home.

Her suit, a fashionable teal green with gold buttons, didn't wrinkle, and though the skirt was narrow, it was short enough for her to maneuver stairs. She'd be fine in it.

The cowboy didn't know what he was talking about. Just like her brothers.

The door opened and the man in her thoughts stood there, his arms full of pillows, blankets and a thermos as well as a duffel bag. "Ready?"

"Yes." She'd already loaded everything she was taking into her car. Her trunk space was minimal. She wasn't even sure his duffel bag would fit.

"Aren't you taking any luggage?"

She sighed. "I've already loaded my things."

"I would've been glad to carry them for you."

She wanted to go ballistic on him, letting him know that a woman could manage on her own. She didn't need a Neanderthal following her around, using his muscles on her behalf. But she realized he was just trying to be polite, even if stereotypical, and instead, she simply said, "Not necessary."

Kathy was just behind her brother. "Gil, be careful, please, and call me after you've gotten home."

"I will." He hesitated, then said, "Say hello to Brad for me. Sorry I couldn't stay to visit with him."

Kathy turned a bright red. "I—I'd rather not say you came. If I do, I'd have to tell him you came because I cried, and he'll be upset."

Lindsay watched the interplay between brother and

sister with curiosity. Kathy's words didn't please Gil, but he didn't argue with her. "Your decision."

"Thanks, Gil. Have a happy Thanksgiving." Kathy hugged her brother's neck, almost dislodging everything he carried. He kissed her cheek and turned to Lindsay.

"Let's go."

Like he was in charge.

"Bye, Kathy. Thanks for taking care of my plants."

"I'll see you in a few days," Kathy agreed with a smile, but the others noted the tears in her eyes.

Lindsay pressed the elevator button, hoping one would arrive quickly. Prolonged goodbyes were difficult, and Kathy seemed to be having problems with this one.

"Go on back in and get some rest, baby. We're on our way," Gil insisted.

"No, I—"

The dinging of a bell signifying the arrival of an elevator stopped her. Lindsay waved and quickly stepped on, followed by Gil.

"Aren't you taking a coat? That jacket doesn't look heavy enough to keep you warm."

Lindsay waited until they reached the lobby. Once she was out of the elevator, out of the confined space with the man, she turned around and faced him. "Let's get something straight before we start. I am not your sister. Nor do I need a keeper. This is my car, my trip. You can come along, as long as you understand I'm in charge! Got it?"

* * *

Gil squared his jaw and considered walking away from this stubborn woman. He could take a hotel room and wait out the storm.

But he really wanted to get home.

Before he made up his mind, she spoke again. "I'm sorry if that sounded rude, but I don't like someone hovering over me. If we're going to be in a car together for fifteen hours, I thought it would be better to clear the air now."

In even tones, hiding his irritation, he said, "Fair enough." Then he stood there, waiting for her to lead the way.

It seemed to take a minute for her to realize he was waiting on her. Snapping her chin into the air, she turned and headed through the door that led to the parking garage.

Again he reconsidered his decision when he saw her car. A Miata. He was going to be trapped in a small car for fifteen hours with a feminist—a touchy feminist—which was like a cowboy being cornered by a bull with a hatred for humans. Unmanageable.

"The trunk is full," she muttered. "But I think all your things can go in the back seat."

What back seat? There was a narrow ledge behind the front two seats. But he wasn't about to argue. He stuffed everything where she said. Then he pulled off his denim, fleece-lined coat and laid it on top. It occurred to him again to ask where her coat was, and whether she shouldn't put it inside the car, too. But there was no way he was risking another pithy lecture.

Then he squeezed himself into the passenger seat. Damn, he was going to feel like a pretzel by the time they reached Oklahoma.

"Please fasten your seat belt," she reminded him.

Oh, yeah, he didn't want to forget that little thing. A woman driver who had taken an instant dislike to him? No, he didn't want to take any *more* chances.

The minute they pulled out of the parking garage into city traffic, Gil knew the trip was going to take longer than expected. The roads were jammed, filled with impatient drivers using their horns to indicate their frustration.

"Crowded today," he said, casually watching Lindsay out of the corner of his eye.

She was frowning, but as far as he could tell, she was in control. "I've never seen it this crowded."

"Well, with the snowstorm and the holiday, I suppose we should've expected it."

"If it's too much for you, Mr. Daniels, you can get out now. It's only a short walk back to the apartment." She made her statement without heat, as if it didn't matter to her either way.

"Hey, I wasn't trying to complain. I was only making a comment. An inoffensive comment."

He watched her fingers tighten on the steering wheel before she released them. "My apology. I guess I'm a little stressed today."

"Understandable. A change of plans at the last minute can be hard to handle."

She gave a hint of a smile that vanished quickly, and she concentrated on her driving.

Gil studied her. She was beautiful enough to satisfy any man. Her blond hair was swept up into some kind of twist, leaving him to wonder how long it was. Her makeup was discreet, enhancing her smooth features. Her hazel eyes were complemented by the color of her suit.

And she had killer legs.

He'd noticed them beneath the short skirt when he was following her to her car.

The rest of her seemed well-proportioned, too, though he couldn't tell much with the long, boxy jacket she wore.

Just the kind of woman he avoided.

Grimly, he pictured his ex-wife. She'd always been on the best-dressed list. Every hair had been in place. Nothing would do but the most expensive for her. Fashion was the most important thing in her life and came before everything else.

Including him. It was demoralizing to come in second to a cashmere sweater set. Ultimately, he just hadn't lived up to Amanda's expectations for a husband.

"Damn!" his companion muttered, catching him by surprise.

"What's wrong?"

They'd been edging their way along Lakeshore Drive. Now even edging had been eliminated. Long lines of traffic had come to a complete halt.

"I'd hoped we could reach Interstate 55 before it got this bad. Surely once we get on that highway, things will move faster."

"Interstate 55. That goes to St. Louis, doesn't it?"

"Yes. From there, we'll take Interstate 44. It goes to Oklahoma City."

"You got a map?" he asked.

Her head snapped around. "I know where I'm going!"

He heaved a sigh. Yep, an angry bull. "I thought I might see if there was another way to get to 55. Lakeshore Drive is pretty famous."

Her cheeks flushed. "Sorry. I'm a little tense about— There's a map of Chicago in the glove compartment."

Was she nervous about being alone with him? She wasn't fainthearted, like his sister, that was for sure. Without comment, he pulled out the map. He noted she had a map of the Midwest in there, also. She was well prepared.

After studying the map, he checked their location. "Have we passed Madison Avenue yet?"

"Not yet. It's coming up."

"We could exit on it. Then just about any road that crosses it will take us to 55."

"You're sure? I've never—"

"We're not moving. Look for yourself." He didn't point out that her doubting his word was as insulting as his telling her what to do.

She took the map from him and studied it. Then, with an apologetic smile, she said, "You're right. Now, if the traffic will only move a little bit, we can get out of this maze."

"Just don't be surprised if half of these drivers have the same idea," he warned her.

"If half of them had the same idea, we'd at least be moving. I'm afraid the snowstorm will catch us before we can get out of town. Look at those clouds."

She gestured over her shoulder and he realized she'd been watching the weather in the rearview mirror.

"Pretty ominous," he agreed, "but maybe it's lake effect clouds. I've heard it can increase the amount of snow. By the time it hits though, we should be out of Chicago."

"I hope so. I think I'll try to catch the latest weather report."

She fiddled with the radio for several minutes, finally settling on one playing music. "I think this station gives a weather report on the hour."

He checked his watch. They'd left at one-thirty and it was already almost two. They'd only gone a few blocks.

The weather report wasn't good. It seemed the storm predicted for that evening had strengthened even more and was picking up speed. Now its estimated time of arrival was three o'clock.

Lindsay moaned.

Gil's stomach clenched. He hadn't been with a woman in a long time, but his wife had made little moans in bed when they'd first married, when making love had been important to her.

He didn't want to be reminded.

"What's making you tense?" he said.

She turned startled eyes on him. "I—what are you asking?"

"When I asked for a map, you said you were tense about something, but you stopped before you finished your sentence."

"I really don't think that's any of your business," she said stiffly.

"I guess not. But it made me curious."

"I didn't offer to satisfy your curiosity. Just to drive you to Oklahoma." She stared straight ahead.

"Fine." He crossed his arms over his chest. He didn't need to listen to her problems anyway. He had some of his own.

"Where in Oklahoma do you live? Is it close to Interstate 44?"

"Yeah, pretty close, but if you get me to any major city, I can catch a flight out."

"With the holiday traffic, that might not be true. What town do you live in?"

"You won't have heard of it. It's a little town south of Oklahoma City. Apache."

"That explains it," she said, a disgusted look on her face.

"Explains what?"

"You wanted to know what was making me tense? It's going home to my brothers."

"You don't like your brothers?" he asked, even as he wondered why they were back on this subject.

"I love my brothers. But they're always bossing me around. Just like you. That's why I'm tense. And we live near Duncan, a few miles from Apache. I guess that's why you remind me of them."

"Then we're even," he replied, his voice tight. "Because you remind me of my ex-wife, Amanda."

She turned to gape at him, her eyes wide, just as the driver behind them sat down on his horn.

The traffic had begun to move.

Gil sighed. It was going to be a long ride home.

Chapter Two

Lindsay glared in her rearview mirror at the impatient driver behind her. Not that she could blame him, but she didn't like his rude reminder.

It made her think of the man sitting next to her.

She inched the car forward. "Why did you say that?"

"Because it's the truth."

"I didn't know you'd been married before. Kathy never mentioned it." She reviewed their conversations about Gil. Kathy had raved about her wonderful brother, but a sister-in-law had never been mentioned.

"You and Kathy discuss me?" His question was abrupt, clipped, as if the idea of her discussing him offended him.

"No, *I* don't discuss you, but Kathy talks about you a lot."

"Maybe the subject didn't come up because Kathy

hated my ex. Especially after the divorce.'' He stared out the window. ''Madison is just ahead.''

His reminder irritated her even more. ''I haven't forgotten.''

Nothing more was said until after she, along with a number of other cars, made the turn onto Madison, but their speed did pick up from a standstill to a slow crawl.

''Why do I remind you of your ex? Kathy and I get along just fine,'' Lindsay said.

''You remind me of my ex because you're wearing a dressy suit to make a fifteen hour drive in less-than-pleasant circumstances.''

Lindsay stared at him. ''Your ex-wife made a lot of long drives in suits?''

''You can go now,'' he said, nodding to the road in front of them, not answering her question.

Lindsay kept her gaze on the road, determined not to be caught lagging again.

She was startled when he actually answered her question. She hadn't expected him to.

''My wife didn't make long drives. But she always insisted on being fashionably dressed no matter what the circumstances.''

Lindsay thought the man was being rather hard on his ex-wife. After all, there was nothing wrong with wanting to look one's best. But she wasn't going to argue with him about it.

''Look at the map and figure out which road it would be best to take to get to the highway,'' she suggested, keeping her gaze on the traffic. ''The sooner we get on the interstate, the better off we'll be.''

"And you're willing to take my word for it?"

She ignored the temptation to glare at him. If she did, she'd get honked at again. Or barked at by her companion.

"Yes."

He studied the map and suggested she take the next crossroad, Central Avenue. It only took a couple of minutes to reach the intersection and make the turn, but she gasped as she swung the car into the appropriate lane.

"What?" he asked sharply, staring at her.

"The snow's here," she muttered, watching a large flake settle against the windshield.

After a moment of silence, he asked, "Want to turn back? Have you changed your mind?"

"No! I'm going on, but you can change *your* mind, if you want."

"Not me. I want to get home."

"Why did you come to Chicago if you hate it here so much?" It wasn't that she didn't understand his attitude toward big cities. Her brothers all reacted the same way, even to Oklahoma City, which couldn't compare to Chicago for traffic jams and hordes of people.

Even she— But she shut that thought away. She couldn't afford to admit her annoyance of Chicago, even to herself.

"Do you know Brad, Kathy's husband?"

The non sequitur surprised her. "Of course I do."

"What do you think of him?"

She studied him out of the corner of her eye even as she paid attention to the traffic. "Why?"

"It's a simple question."

"Don't *you* know Brad?"

"Barely. I've met him a couple of times. Once at the wedding, and a couple of hours last Christmas."

"And you don't like him." She wasn't asking a question. The man's attitude toward his brother-in-law was evident.

"I don't know him."

"And that's why you asked *my* opinion? A woman who reminds you of your ex?"

"Forget it." He turned to stare out his window again.

But she couldn't. "He seems nice enough. Devoted to Kathy."

"Yeah?" he asked with a big frown. "He hasn't—hit on you?"

"Me? You think he'd hit on me, living across from his wife?" She was astounded. Even if Brad had been the type to mess around, she wasn't. "Even if he had, I would never—"

"Kathy called me yesterday. Crying."

"And you thought—"

"I didn't know what to think. She wouldn't tell me what was wrong. I flew up this morning to see if there was anything I could do. She still wouldn't tell me. But you heard her. She didn't want to tell Brad I'd come."

She should've known. He'd already reminded her of her brothers by his dress. Now he reminded her of her brothers with his protectiveness, his smothering of his sister.

"Look, all married couples go through some rough patches. They have to work things out themselves. You can't fix everything just because she's your little sister." She tried to keep her voice calm, but she heard it tightening as she finished speaking.

"Thank you, Dr. Joyce Brothers."

His sarcastic reply only irritated her more. If it had been left to her brothers, she would've sat upon a silken pillow all her days and never even learned to walk, much less fend for herself. That's why she'd been forced to leave home. She hadn't realized she and Kathy had that much in common.

Time to concentrate on her driving. This cowboy wouldn't appreciate her opinion any more than her brothers had.

"Have you ever heard them fighting?"

"No." In fact, she'd been a little envious of Kathy. Not that she was attracted to Brad, but she was attracted to the devotion the two shared, the closeness. Since she'd moved away from home, she'd sometimes longed for a relationship that could lead to marriage.

As long as the man understood she wouldn't be smothered.

She was glad she was concentrating on her driving when they got up on the interstate. As she increased her speed, her tires began to spin and the back end of the car skidded a little. She immediately eased up on the gas.

"Better keep your speed down," her companion advised.

"Really? Are you sure I shouldn't go faster?"

His head snapped around to stare at her.

"I was being sarcastic," she pointed out, as if speaking to a slow learner.

"Oh. Thanks for explaining."

She shrugged her shoulders. Okay, so two could be sarcastic. Maybe she'd deserved that kind of answer. She turned her windshield wipers up to high speed as the snow began coming down faster. She'd be glad when the highway turned farther south. It was their only hope of outrunning the storm.

Gil didn't make any more attempts at conversation. It had been foolish to try to soothe his concerns about Kathy by asking Lindsay questions. Like he'd trust her evaluation anyway. A woman who dressed in a designer suit to drive in a snowstorm.

His ex-wife had been impressed with anyone with money. Their morals, or intelligence or even their warmth had no value compared to their bank account.

He knew Brad made a good living. But he wanted his sister to be happy, not well dressed. He wanted her husband to love her, not buy her things. Well, he wanted him to buy her things, too, but that wasn't the most important. He didn't want Kathy to wind up in the same kind of loveless marriage that he had.

As Lindsay carefully steered the car, Gil studied her hands. They looked smooth, soft, but he was surprised by her nails. While well tended, they weren't long, and the polish was clear. She only wore one ring, an opal with diamonds.

"Nice ring. A gift?"

"Yes."

Aha. So she had some man on a string, willing to buy her expensive things. He remembered when he'd first fallen for Amanda. He'd prided himself on buying her what she wanted. Until he realized that was all she wanted. Real emotions—even love—meant nothing to her.

When Lindsay gasped again, he brought his attention back to the road. A car that had just passed by them went into a spin. It narrowly missed going over the side as it came to rest against the railing.

"You okay?" he asked, studying her to determine whether she would be able to continue driving.

"Yes," she said with a sigh. "Should we stop to help them?"

"There's not a lot we could do. Unless you want to call 911 for them."

"My cell phone is in my purse. Could you call for me? I want to concentrate on my driving."

He found the phone and called in the near accident. After hanging up, he said, "They promised to send a cop to check on them."

"Thank you."

"They were going too fast," he added.

She sent him a look that told him she got his less than subtle message. But, in truth, she was keeping her speed down. In fact, she was doing a good job with her driving, though he hated to admit it.

He checked his watch. It was already after three. They'd been driving almost two hours and hadn't gotten out of Chicago yet.

She must've caught his movement out of the corner of her eye because she asked, "What time is it?"

"Almost three-thirty."

Though she frowned, she didn't say anything.

He settled more comfortably in his seat. "If you get tired of driving, I can spell you."

She didn't answer for a minute. Then she said, "They don't get much snow in Oklahoma."

So she doubted his skills? "I lived in New York for almost ten years."

"In New York City? I didn't think many people drove in the city."

"We had a house in upstate New York, spent weekends there, particularly in the winter because of the skiing." He'd enjoyed the skiing. But he hadn't enjoyed the collection of people his wife invited to join them. They'd been her friends, not his.

"I guess you don't get much skiing in Apache."

"Nope. But I've made several trips to Colorado since I moved back."

"What do you do for a living?"

"Ranching."

"In New York City?" she asked, her voice rising in surprise.

"No, not in New York City. I was a stockbroker there." And he'd been one of the best. Which had made it possible for him to come back to Oklahoma and buy his ranch, even after the divorce.

"Do you miss being a stockbroker?"

"Nope." Which was the truth, but he didn't mention that he still bought and sold stocks, managing his personal fortune. He was also doing some investing for Rafe, his ranch manager, who had become a good friend and a mentor. Gil wanted to make it possible for Rafe to achieve his own dream.

Staring out the window, he realized the snow was getting thicker. "Can you still see well enough to keep going? Maybe we should stop while we can still find a hotel and wait until morning." He didn't want to do that, but he also didn't want to become a frozen Popsicle on the side of the road.

"No, I want to keep going. I have snow tires on my car." She leaned forward to concentrate on her driving, and Gil figured she'd be sore before too long. The tension would make her ache.

He said nothing. She'd probably offer to dump him out on the closest sidewalk if he protested. And he had to admit they could still maneuver fairly well. But he wasn't sure how long that would be true.

An hour later, they were still struggling along, the snow several inches deep. He'd pulled his sheepskin-lined jacket into the front seat and draped it over himself. Lindsay, though occasionally shivering, said nothing.

He felt like a cur, sitting back and warm while she shivered and drove through the storm, but he'd offered to drive. And he'd asked her about her coat. And she'd responded to both those questions with a snarl.

So he kept quiet.

"I'm sure we'll be clear of the snow if we can just get to St. Louis," she said suddenly.

"I won't argue with that," he agreed, but he had his doubts about making it that far.

"Or even Springfield," she added, sending him a hopeful look.

He stared straight ahead. Then they passed a sign showing an exit for a town named Pontiac. "How far is Pontiac from Springfield?"

"I'm—I'm not sure."

He opened the glove compartment and took out the larger map covering the Midwest. After a brief calculation, he looked at her. "I believe it's over eighty miles."

She pressed her lips tightly together and said nothing.

Neither did he, but he didn't think they'd make it eighty miles before midnight. Not when they were only going about fifteen miles an hour.

Finally, he said, "I'm willing to pull over and find a place to stay to wait this out, whenever you're ready. You know we're not going to be able to drive straight through at this rate."

She shook her head. "We'll be able to go a lot faster as soon as we outrun the snowstorm."

Stubborn woman. He couldn't argue with her statement. In fact, he totally agreed with her. The disagreement came in exactly when they'd outrun the snowstorm.

"Mind if I turn on the radio?" he asked. "We might get some weather news."

"No, of course not. That's a good idea." She reached for the radio herself.

"I'll handle the radio, since you're driving." He thought he'd put that tactfully, and her hand returned to the steering wheel, leaving it to him to find a station.

"This is a weather bulletin," the announcer said. "Forecasters say the storm will still intensify for the next few hours. However, the snow should taper off by morning."

"By morning!" Lindsay exclaimed.

Gil said nothing. He didn't think urging Lindsay to give up would be effective. The hardheaded woman would probably refuse to do so because she didn't want to give in to a man's advice. He understood a woman's resistance to male domination, but not in the face of common sense.

"Lindsay, the snow's almost half a foot deep now. We're not going to be able to go much farther. Don't you want to look for shelter while we can?" he finally asked.

She said nothing, leaning farther over the steering wheel, her gaze glued to the road in front of them.

Gil sighed.

Abruptly, she put on her blinker light, taking him by surprise. "You're stopping?" he asked.

Though her face remained grim, she nodded. "There's a small town here, according to that sign. I guess we'd better stop while we can."

"Good thinking," he agreed, as if it had been her idea. He didn't care who got credit for stopping, as long as they did so.

The exit road was downhill and they skidded several times negotiating it. When they reached the bottom, they discovered another sign, pointing out that the small town they'd sought was another four miles down the road.

"Rats!" Lindsay exclaimed, frowning fiercely.

"We can make it," Gil assured her. Four miles on level road would be a hell of a lot better than trying to go uphill to get back on the freeway.

"We don't have much choice," she muttered, not looking at him.

"Want me to drive?"

She glared at him. "No."

He drew a deep breath and leaned back, trying to give the impression of complete relaxation.

Half an hour later, they reached the city limits of Witherspoon.

"Where is it?" Lindsay demanded in frustration.

"I think I see a few buildings. Keep going."

He was right. They discovered a filling station, obviously shut down, a Dairy Queen, no lights on, a couple of houses and finally the red fluorescent light appeared through the snow, flashing OTEL.

"I think we can assume that should say motel," he said with a chuckle.

"I hope you're right." She turned off the road into the parking lot.

Gil studied as much as he could see of the motel and figured they'd be lucky to get a room. The parking lot was almost full.

"There's the office," he said, pointing to their right.

She eased the car through the crunchy snow and stopped as close to the office door as she could.

"If you'd like, I'll go see what they've got available. I've already got my coat out," he offered, careful to couch his idea as a suggestion.

"Thank you. I'd appreciate it."

Surprised by her acquiescence without argument, he hurriedly got out into the storm before she could change her mind.

The cold sting of the snow attacked his exposed skin as he hurried toward the door, trying not to slip.

As soon as he got inside, closing the door behind him, he shook off the snow that covered him and stepped to the counter.

No one appeared to be on duty, but there was a button to push for assistance. After he'd followed

directions, he heard footsteps. Then, a door behind
the counter opened and an elderly man appeared.

"Evening. Didn't hear anyone arrive. Sorry to
keep you waiting," he said, a genial smile on his
face. "We don't usually do this much business."

Gil would guess not. So far he hadn't seen anything in Witherspoon that would attract travelers. Of
course, he hadn't seen much in the snowstorm, so he
could be wrong.

"You're in luck," the man said. "I've got one
room left. You want it?"

Gil frowned. "Only one room? We need two."

"Sorry, young man. But one's all I got. If you
don't want it, someone else will probably come
along."

Gil felt sure he was right. "Is there another motel
in town?"

"Nope. This is it."

The sound of another vehicle on the road just
barely penetrated the room above the sound of the
wind. Gil didn't want to do any more driving in the
storm. He hurriedly agreed to the one room, pulling
out his credit card.

"We, uh, had to up the price a little, because of
the storm, you know. Had to hire extra help to get
all the rooms ready." The man avoided Gil's cynical
gaze.

He wasn't surprised to discover price-gouging. It
happened all the time. In fact, he figured the man
had a hard time making a living wage most days.

He waited for the man to run his credit card, thinking about the reaction he was bound to receive when

he announced to Lindsay Crawford that they were going to share a motel room.

The man handed over an old-fashioned key. None of those fancy plastic cards that the hotels used these days. Gil almost smiled as he pocketed the key. Just as he put his hand on the door to venture out into the storm, he looked over his shoulder. "This room does have two beds, doesn't it?"

The man stared at him, and Gil got a sinking feeling in his stomach.

Chapter Three

Lindsay shivered as the wind swirled around the car, making visibility impossible. She was glad they'd stopped, but she wished they could continue on. She wished she had her coat out of the trunk. She wished... A blur of movement stopped her thoughts.

Suddenly the passenger door opened and Gil slid into the car, bringing with him snow and wind. She shivered again.

"Okay," he said, not looking at her. "We need to turn right. Room number nine."

Without speaking, she followed his directions, forcing her car to push its way through the snow. They could barely make out the numbers on the doors of the single story structure. There was a parking space in front of number nine and she pulled her car into it.

Then it occurred to her that he'd only given her the number of one room.

"Is this your room or mine?"

Dead silence. He didn't even look at her.

"Gil? Is this—"

"Our room."

It was her turn to be silent.

His gaze met hers. "He only had one room left. We can't go on, and we can't stay in the car. I didn't know what to do but take the room. I promise you you're in no danger from me."

She believed him. And she should've been grateful. She *was* grateful, she hurriedly assured herself. But he needn't make it sound so easy.

All afternoon, closed up in her small car, his male aura had kept her aware, tense…interested, no matter how much she told herself she wasn't attracted to him.

Now she was going to share a motel room with him?

And he assured her that wouldn't be a problem.

What could she say? He was right. They couldn't go any farther. And neither of them could stay in the car. He'd done the only practical thing. After drawing a deep breath, she said, "Thanks, I appreciate your assurance."

He stared at her, as if her reaction differed from what he'd expected. "You mean you're not going to insist I sleep in the car?"

"And have your death on my hands? Of course not. I can share a room with you for the night." So he'd be sleeping a few feet away. Maybe she'd have trouble getting to sleep, but she was tired. She'd manage.

"Great. We'd better take these blankets I borrowed from Kathy. We might need them."

Normal, practical words. So why was he avoiding her gaze? Why was she waiting for the other shoe to drop? Something wasn't right, but for the life of her, she couldn't imagine what it could be.

"Okay. Did the clerk mention anything about where we could get supper?"

"He's got a small grocery attached to the office. Not a lot of selection, but I'll go back and find something as soon as we get settled in the room. And there's a microwave we can use, too."

"In the room?" she asked, surprised by a modern convenience like a microwave in a 1950s motel.

He grinned. "Nope. In the office. The food will probably be cold before I can get it to the room, but hopefully it won't be frozen. There is a coffee machine in the room, though."

"I'll start a pot at once," she promised. "Can you get the blankets and your bag? I need to get my bag and coat out of the trunk."

"Sure. Need some help?"

"No, thank you."

By the time she'd struggled through the wind and snow, retrieved her belongings and made it to the door of their room, she wished she hadn't been quite so fiercely independent. She could admit to herself, if not to her companion, that it would've been really nice to run for the door and leave the carrying to Gil's strong shoulders.

He was waiting for her and immediately closed the door behind her, shutting out the storm.

She covered her face with her hands, grateful to feel the warmth against her chilled cheeks. "Thanks," she muttered, leaning against the wall.

"It's brutal out there. And you didn't get your coat on."

"It seemed easier just to gather it up and run," she said, raising her head and smiling wearily at Gil.

Over his shoulder, she took in the room.

"I see our room is as out of date as—"

When her gaze focused on the major piece of furniture in the small room, she couldn't continue. She just stared at it instead.

Then she stared at Gil.

"You're not surprised," she accused.

He turned to look at the double bed. As if to remind himself of what she'd discovered. "No, I'm not. The clerk told me there was only one bed. But I was hoping for king-size."

"What are we going to do?" Sudden visions of sharing the bed with Gil, a large man, and sexy as could be, left her mouth dry.

"We're going to get some sleep. And I promise that's all we're going to do, so don't give me any virginal protests. You're safe."

Of course she was. The dratted man had made it more than clear he had no interest in her. But was she safe from herself?

"You could sleep on the floor," she suggested, finding the air suddenly thin.

"So could you. I thought you were a feminist,

wanting to prove you're as strong as any guy. Want to draw for the bed?''

The immediate outrage that filled her had her reconsider her reaction. He was right. She'd fought for being equal to her brothers, but when things got difficult she wanted special treatment?

"No. There's no point in either of us being uncomfortable. We'll share." If he could control himself, she was sure she could do the same. She hoped. It wasn't as if she had an uncontrollable libido. In fact, she'd never understood others' fascination with sex.

But the itchiness she'd been feeling all afternoon in the car, because of this man, had her reevaluating her previous experience.

"The bathroom is, uh, pretty small, too," Gil said, as if giving her the rest of the bad news now that she'd remained calm about the bed.

She moved to the door just past the bed and peeked into the bath. Gil had understated its size. Postage stamp might be more accurate. No tub. Only a small shower, sink and toilet. So much for the thought of a hot, soaking bath.

More shivers brought her attention to another disappointment. The room wasn't warm.

"Is the heater on? Can we turn it up? I'm still cold," she said, looking around the room.

"It's a lot warmer than outside, but definitely not toasty," Gil agreed. He crossed the room to the small controls on the wall by the door. Sighing, he turned to face her. "I'm afraid it's on high."

Lindsay moaned in disappointment.

* * *

Damn, she had to stop making that noise. It made Gil think of long nights of mindless sex. Which warmed him up a little in spite of the inadequacies of the furnace.

He turned his mind to food, a safer subject than sex. Especially since he'd given his word that he'd keep his hands off of her. He hoped he hadn't been overly optimistic. After all, she was a beauty.

She'd surprised him with her calm acceptance not only of the one room but also the one bed. He'd expected a tantrum, like Amanda had been capable of. She'd demanded luxury no matter what the circumstances.

"Want to give me some idea of what you want for dinner?" he asked, waiting for a long list of preferences.

She actually grinned at him. "I don't eat liver. I'm not fond of fish—or spinach. Anything else is fine. And I wouldn't say no to a candy bar. Stress makes me crave chocolate."

He couldn't resist tracing her slim form with his gaze. She must normally live a stress-free life. Otherwise she'd be several sizes larger. Which made her agreeableness even more amazing. He'd been attracted to her beauty from the beginning. Now, he was drawn to that grin, that twinkle in her hazel eyes.

"I'll see what I can find."

"Wait!" she called out as he turned to the door.

Before he knew what she intended, she'd looped a red cashmere scarf around his neck. "I noticed you didn't have a muffler. This will keep your face warm," she assured him as she tied it.

Her arms were around his neck, securing the scarf

and he froze, aware that it wouldn't take much movement to pull her into his embrace, to warm her body with his. But he didn't move. He'd promised.

Against the soft cloth, he muttered, "I'll be right back."

He stepped out into the storm, scarcely noting the frigid conditions. It reminded him of that song, "Let It Snow," with the words that said the singer would stay warm if he got a hug before he left.

He'd always laughed at that silliness, but even the thought of an embrace from Lindsay had him steaming.

He returned a few minutes later with a variety of food, none of it gourmet. He'd nuked several prepackaged hamburgers in the microwave, picked up the last two egg salad sandwiches wrapped in cellophane, grabbed a couple of bags of chips and selected several chocolate candy bars.

Lindsay deserved any treat he could find.

When he burst into the motel room, slamming the door behind him, he was immediately assailed by the aroma of hot coffee. "You made the coffee!" he exclaimed.

"I said I would," she replied. "I figured it might be the only way we'll get warm tonight. In fact, I might even soak my feet in coffee later on. They feel like blocks of ice."

He swallowed his "told you so" thought about the shoes she'd chosen to wear. No point in starting an argument when they had an entire night to get through together. "Want to see what's for dinner?"

"Yes," she said, coming around the bed.

He pulled the two hamburgers from inside his

coat. "These are still warm, but we'd better eat them fast. These sandwiches are the second course. Chips to accompany either or both. And, ta-da," he called, as if presenting the pièce de résistance, "chocolate for dessert."

"Bless you," she said, taking her share of his offerings.

Gil hadn't believed she'd be pleased with his selections. Pleased? Hell, he'd expected her to turn her nose up at all of it.

She surprised him even more when she put her food down and returned to the other side of the bed to pour both of them a cup of coffee before starting to eat.

"Warm is more than I expected. With the coffee, they might even taste hot." She set his cup on the lamp table, then moved down the length of the bed and sat down.

Neither bothered with conversation while they ate. By the time Gil took the last bite of his hamburger, it was cold, but the coffee was still warm. And the egg salad sandwich helped satisfy his hunger.

Lindsay handed him the second half of hers. "I'm saving room for the chocolate. You finish mine off."

"Don't mind if I do," he said with a grin. Before he ate any of it, however, he added, "Thanks for being such a good sport about all this, Lindsay."

She looked surprised. "Why not be a good sport? None of it is your fault. In fact, if I'd stopped when you first suggested it, our accommodations might be a little more...spacious." She shrugged her shoulders. "You're the one who should be complaining."

Rather than argue about who was responsible for

their situation, he smiled and finished off her sandwich.

"Do you think we'll be able to get any reception on the television?" she asked, eyeing the set against the wall.

"Maybe. It looks remarkably new compared to everything else in the room." He set down his coffee cup and crossed over to the television. When he turned it on, Lindsay cheered as a clear picture filled the screen.

"All right! My favorite show comes on tonight," she said.

Gil changed the channel, only to discover that only one station got reception. "Then I hope it's on this channel."

"Me, too. If you don't mind, I'm going to take a turn in the bathroom."

With a nod, he watched her grab her suitcase and open it, extracting several articles. Then she tucked it away and disappeared into the bath.

All he could think about was Lindsay emerging in something from Victoria Secret. A man could dream, couldn't he?

When Lindsay finally opened the door, she was completely dressed in a velour warm-up suit, with thick socks on her feet. She sent him a nervous grin. "Not the latest style in pj's, but this is the warmest I have."

"I think you look very stylish," he assured her. When she frowned at him, he asked, "What?"

"Is that a slam?"

"Why would you think that?"

"You said your ex-wife always had to be in style."

Gil was at a loss at what to say. His first reaction was to tell her his wife wouldn't have been caught dead in a sweat suit—unless she was modeling it in a fashion show. But that response wouldn't do. The alternative was to tell her that he thought she'd look stylish in a trash bag, because all he'd be able to think about was what was underneath.

That *definitely* wouldn't do.

"Uh, I was teasing you. Being warm is a lot more important than being stylish."

She smiled and picked up two of the candy bars. Then she returned to the side of the bed closest to the bathroom and pulled down the covers. "I'm getting under the covers to watch television."

He stood and moved his candy bars to the lamp table. "Good idea. Want a refill on the coffee? I think there's just enough for both of us."

"Sure, thanks."

After filling their cups, he gathered his duffel bag and, with a nod of his head in the direction of the bathroom, he walked past her, closing the door behind him.

Lindsay drew a deep breath when she was finally alone. The man, with his sexy grin, was tough to resist. She couldn't even suggest he sleep in the tub tonight, because there wasn't one.

Oh, well. She could share the bed with him. After all, he'd brought her chocolate. She unwrapped the candy and took a big bite. Then she turned her pillow on end and sank into it, focusing her gaze on the television.

If there had been more covers, so she could really get warm, Lindsay thought she might've even drifted off to sleep, though it was barely eight o'clock. But the two thin blankets on the bed didn't provide much warmth.

When the bathroom door swung open and Gil came back into her view, she felt the room get suddenly a little warmer. He was still dressed in jeans, but he'd changed his cotton shirt to a flannel one, left open over a white T-shirt.

"You're going to sleep in jeans?" she asked, frowning.

He cocked one eyebrow at her. "I only brought jeans."

She thought about his words as he pulled back the covers on his side of the bed. She knew he'd be uncomfortable, but he could sleep if he was really tired. She'd done it before when she'd been camping out with the family.

"You'll probably need them. These blankets aren't much help."

He snapped his fingers. "I forgot about the ones I borrowed from Kathy." He reached for the blankets that he'd dumped in a corner of the room and spread them out over the bed.

Lindsay immediately felt the difference. "Oh, thank you for thinking of them. That helps a lot."

Even more effective at raising her temperature was Gil's entry into the bed. His body heat was like a personal furnace, even though he maintained the foot of distance that the size of the bed allowed.

Twelve inches. And those twelve inches were possible only because she'd scooted to the edge of the bed. Gil's broad shoulders took up more than his half of the bed. The temptation to press her body against his, resting her head on his shoulder, was almost overpowering.

"You're not going to fall off the bed, are you?"

She snapped her head around. "Of course not! But I wanted you to have enough room."

"I appreciate it," he assured her with a grin that could compete with Mel Gibson's any day.

She forced her gaze back to the television. A movie had just started. It wasn't the show she'd anticipated, but it was one she hadn't seen. Beggars couldn't be choosers. At least it might distract her from the sexy man next to her.

Two hours later, the movie ended, and Lindsay tried to unobtrusively wipe away the tears that had filled her eyes. She was always a sucker for sad stories. Or happy ones. She even cried over Hallmark commercials.

"You okay?" a quiet, tender voice asked.

"Of course!" she exclaimed, irritated that he'd noticed her tears. She shoved back the covers and jumped out of bed. "But I have to brush my teeth before I can go to sleep." She grabbed her toothbrush and toothpaste and disappeared into the bathroom, shutting the door behind her.

Gil lay back against his pillow, missing the heat from Lindsay's body almost at once. The room wasn't much warmer than when they'd first entered it. He supposed there was too much demand for heat from the system.

Not that he'd been cold. No, with Lindsay in bed beside him, so close, he'd been warm. Aroused, but warm. He now had the answer about how long her hair was. When she'd come out of the bathroom, he'd been too distracted by the total picture to pay attention to detail. But she'd taken all the pins out and brushed it and it hung in silken strands to her shoulders. The urge to stroke it was very distracting.

Maybe that was why it had taken him a while to realize she was crying over the sentimental film. At first he'd been amused. Then touched. Suddenly, the need to hold her, comfort her, had turned to raging hormones. The thought of pulling her into his arms was too tempting.

Good thing she'd gone to brush her teeth.

When she came back out, he took his turn in the bathroom. If he stayed in there long enough, maybe she'd fall asleep before he came back.

It was too cold and uncomfortable to stay in the bathroom longer than five minutes. He cautiously opened the door, flicking off the light quickly so it wouldn't shine in Lindsay's eyes.

But she'd left the bedside lamp on for him. He stared at her rigid form, strictly on her side of the bed. She definitely wasn't asleep.

"The coffee keeping you awake?" he whispered.

"Um, I don't think so. I used decaffeinated. It's probably the chocolate. It has caffeine, too, you know."

Now she told him. He'd have limited her to one candy bar if he'd thought of that. He rounded the bed and slipped beneath the covers again. His side of the bed had grown cold, but he could feel Lindsay's heat.

"Are you still cold?" she whispered as a shiver racked him.

"I'll warm up in a minute. It doesn't take long for the bed to get cold, does it?" His own words reminded him of his marriage. Once the ring was on Amanda's finger, her eagerness to share a bed with him had vanished. She'd made it very clear she was more interested in his bankroll than his body right away. In fact, their marriage bed had been colder every night than the one he shared with Lindsay tonight.

"Do you have enough room?" she asked, still whispering.

"Yeah." He'd like less room. He'd like Lindsay snuggled up next to him, with no space between. But he'd promised. Gradually, the heat the two of them generated helped him relax.

Until he turned over and found himself facing her, her features barely visible in the dark. "Uh, good night."

"Good night," she said softly.

He turned back over, unable to face her, knowing only inches separated their lips. Hell, it was going to be a long night!

Chapter Four

When Lindsay first stirred the next morning, a sigh of contentment sifted through her and she burrowed her face against Gil's chest, hoping to postpone the inevitable. She didn't want to leave her nice, warm cocoon.

Then she realized what she was lying on. Gil's chest.

She gasped and shoved on the big, warm body that cradled her against him. "Gil!" she snapped.

Accusations stopped up in her throat as he came awake. How could she accuse him of anything when he was still sleeping?

"What?" he muttered, his eyes still closed. In fact, he pulled her closer to him. "Don't move. You're letting in a draft."

She scrambled away from him, pushing against his hands. "Gil! We—you were supposed to stay on your side!"

He slowly opened his eyes, their bright blue a little foggy, as if he awoke slowly. "My side?"

She said nothing, waiting until her words pierced his head.

He frowned, staring at her. Suddenly he jerked his hands from her body and she felt cold.

"Uh, I didn't know. I mean, I must've—it was cold."

His ridiculous words made her reaction seem a little over the top. With a grimace, she said, "So I've heard."

"Really, I know I promised, but I didn't—"

"It's okay, Gil," she said, a calm settling over her. "What time is it?" Even as she asked, she looked at her watch. Nine o'clock!

She looked up to tell him how late they'd slept, only to find him staring at her, shock on his face.

"What? Is my hair standing on end?"

As if he couldn't help himself, he reached out and stroked a strand of hair behind her ear. "No. It's beautiful."

Lying in bed with a man who touched her hair with such awe made her nervous. Because she wanted to return the favor. His dark hair wasn't smooth and in place. But the idea of running her fingers through it held a lot of appeal.

"Um, I'll take first turn in the bathroom. Okay?"

He nodded and she slipped out from under the covers. Away from Gil.

The bed wasn't nearly as warm without Lindsay curled up against him. Or as exciting.

Better stow that thought away. He was going to

have to abandon the covers that hid his reaction to waking up with his arms wrapped around Lindsay. He checked his own watch. A little after nine. He hadn't slept that late in years.

But he'd gladly stay in bed all day if she were with him.

He shook his head in disgust. It was only lust. He hadn't been with a woman since his divorce. He'd have to start getting out more. That would take care of the problem.

The bathroom door opened and Lindsay walked back in the room, wearing what she'd slept in.

"Your turn," she said brightly, as if she were the social director for a cruise line.

"Thanks. You going to wear that today?"

Her cheeks flushed, making her look that much more tempting. "Yes. I have a limited wardrobe and this is the warmest thing I brought."

"Hey, I wasn't complaining," he said at once. "I think it's a smart decision. I'm doing the same thing." He headed for the bathroom before he could say anything else he shouldn't.

When he came back out, Lindsay was on the phone. "Sorry for the delay, Mom, but we should be there this evening, kind of late."

She said her goodbyes and hung up the phone.

"Your mom was worried about you?"

"I suppose, though she seldom shows it. I guess that comes from raising five boys before she got to me."

He chuckled. "You must've been a real shock."

She smiled back. "Why do you think I was the last child? My brothers always claimed my parents stopped because they were afraid they might have another girl, and one was all they could handle.''

He shook his head at her silliness. ''I'd better call Rafe, too. I talked to him before I left Kathy's, but he'll be wondering about me.''

After he hung up the phone, she asked, ''Who's Rafe?''

''My manager. My teacher. I could already ride, but I didn't know much about running a ranch when I first came back to Oklahoma.''

''From New York City?''

''Yeah.''

''That was quite a change of vocation, from stock-broker to rancher.''

He nodded, but he didn't give any explanation. ''You ready to go? We probably should get on the road, if it's open.''

''Will the man in the office know?''

''Probably.''

They loaded their bags back into the car. Another two inches had fallen during the night, but Lindsay managed to get her car started and inch their way to the office.

When she opened her car door as he did his, he looked at her. ''Are you coming in?''

''Yes. I have to pay.''

''I told you I'd pay the expenses of the trip if you'd let me come with you.''

''But you didn't know it would be this long a trip. There's no need—''

''Stay here,'' he ordered. ''I'll ask about the roads.''

Assuming she would obey, he got out of the car.

When he heard the other car door slam, he knew he'd miscalculated.

She'd actually begun to like him! But now he'd resorted back to that typical male behavior. Me, Tarzan, you Jane, and you do what I say!

She beat him to the office door. Or maybe he'd let her beat him. She didn't care, as long as she was the first one inside.

"Morning, Miss. You wantin' a room?" the clerk asked, a smile on his weathered face.

"No, I have a room. We were in number nine last night."

"Oh, right, a'course. I recognize the mister," he said, nodding in Gil's direction.

"Are the roads open this morning?" she asked, ignoring his acknowledgment of her traveling companion.

"Yes, Ma'am. Heard the snowplow go by about seven. Which direction you heading?"

"South," Gil answered before she could.

"No problem, then. Not much snow fifty miles south of here. You'll be fine."

She opened her purse to pull out her credit card as relief filled her. She didn't think she could stand another hour in that small room with Gil.

"Shall I charge it to your card?" the man asked.

Both Gil and she answered with a yes, until she realized what he meant. He was referring to the card Gil had used last night.

"No, I mean, I have my card."

"Don't need but one," the man said calmly.

Gil took her arm. "Don't be difficult, Lindsay. Let's just get on the road."

She glared at him, but there was no relenting in his gaze and the man behind the counter thought she was crazy. She jerked her arm from Gil's hold and stomped to the door.

"Any place for a hot breakfast nearby?" Gil asked before he followed her.

"There's a real good café just down the road. Stay on the side road for another mile. The Roadrunner Café."

"Thanks."

Back in the car, still angry about his high-handedness, Lindsay pulled out onto the highway, keeping her gaze straight ahead.

"If you don't mind, I'd like some breakfast before we get started."

She shot him a dark look. "Aren't you going to order me to stop?"

"Nope. If you want to starve to death, I suppose I can keep you company." He crossed his arms across his chest and stared straight ahead.

She knew she was being ridiculous. "Fine, we'll stop for breakfast. But I'm paying for our food since you paid for the room. And for dinner last night."

"Lady, you may regret that. I like a big breakfast." Instead of arguing, he grinned at her.

"Room nine, please."

The clerk scratched his head. "Uh, sorry, but they checked out about ten minutes ago."

He wondered if the person had hung up, since the caller said nothing. Then the man growled, "They?"

"Yep. There was two of 'em."

"Two women?"

"Nope, a man and his missus. A pretty blonde." He looked at the credit card slip. "A Mr. Daniels."

"I'll kill him," the man exclaimed and slammed down the phone.

"Mercy, I'm glad those people are gone. Don't want no trouble around here." He settled back into his lumpy chair to watch the television.

Lindsay still hadn't warmed up to her companion by the time they'd finished their meal. True, he'd ordered an enormous amount of food. And remained cheerful in spite of her silence.

A lowering thought occurred to her. Was she trying to build a barrier between them, to help her pretend last night hadn't happened? Was she that much of a coward?

"You going to eat that last piece of bacon?" he asked, piercing her thoughts.

She stared at him. "You can't still be hungry?"

"Well, not hungry exactly," he confessed, his gaze sweeping over all the empty plates around him, "but I hate to see a piece of good bacon go to waste."

She silently shoved her plate in his direction. He reminded her of her brothers again. A vacuum cleaner when it came to food.

But she hadn't been thinking of her brothers when she'd awakened this morning wrapped in his arms. In fact, what she'd been thinking would have her father and brothers up in arms. According to them, she should reach her thirtieth birthday unkissed. Then they'd take a vote on allowing her within a mile of any man.

When she realized her gaze had settled on Gil's firm lips, she hurriedly looked away. The couple at the next table drew her attention. The man was hiding behind a newspaper. His wife, or at least she assumed the woman was his wife, was frantically attending to four children, ranging in age from two to maybe ten.

Even as she watched, the two-year-old slid down from his chair and made good his escape, his route bringing him right by Lindsay and Gil. The mother shouted an order, which, of course, the child promptly ignored. However, it alerted Gil to the situation. As junior sped by, he extended his big arm and scooped the child into his lap.

"Whoa, little guy! Where are you heading?"

The child squirmed, but was unable to free himself. Gil's grin seemed to reassure him, though, so the scream of outrage Lindsay expected didn't materialize.

The woman immediately left her chair to claim her child. "Oh, thank you so much. Buster doesn't like to sit still for long." The woman, once pretty, looked tired and too busy to concern herself with her appearance.

The man lowered the paper and scowled at all of them. "Alice, can't you control these kids?"

"Of course, dear," the woman muttered. Then she thanked Gil again and returned to her table, Buster in tow.

"That man should be shot," Lindsay whispered.

She hated men who didn't participate in raising the children they'd fathered.

"Yeah."

Her gaze jerked to Gil's face. She hadn't expected him to agree with her.

Correctly interpreting her response, he said in a low voice, "Why does that surprise you?"

"I didn't think— You seem irritated by my 'feminist' reactions."

He grinned. "That's because sometimes you get carried away. But a man should take care of his children."

While she might want to argue his first statement, she didn't because of his second. She couldn't agree more. "Are you—do you want children?"

His gaze hardened. "No. I wouldn't mind having kids, but that requires a wife. And I won't go down that road again."

Ah, yes. The wife. The one she reminded him of. Somehow that thought hurt more than it had the first time she'd heard it. "Too bad," she said. "You'd make a great daddy."

"Was your father a good daddy?"

"The best," she assured him, a smile on her lips. Then her expression darkened. "Until I became a teenager. Then he and all my brothers became jailers rather than family."

He wiped his mouth with his napkin. "Maybe a slight exaggeration," he suggested.

Before she could argue, the waitress appeared at their table. "Anything else, folks? More coffee?"

"I wouldn't mind a cup to go," Gil suggested. "How about you, Lindsay? Coffee?"

"Yes, a cup to go would be nice. And the ticket, please." She was ready to get on the road, to concentrate on her driving instead of the man across from her. To forget about waking in his arms.

They sat silently until the waitress returned, two foam cups and the ticket in her hands. In spite of Lindsay's having asked for it, the woman presented it to Gil with a smile.

"I'll take that," Lindsay insisted, reaching for the ticket. The waitress looked surprised, but Gil didn't protest at all.

Lindsay put the piece of paper with her credit card and handed it to the woman, ignoring the way her eyebrow went up in question. She muttered something and hurried away.

"What did she say?"

Gil sent her a teasing look. "You're not going to like it. Why don't you just forget she said anything."

Which, of course, only made her more determined to know the waitress's comment. "Tell me."

He straightened his shoulders. "She said she guessed I was worth it."

Lindsay knew he was teasing, pretending to be proud that the waitress rated him worth the price of breakfast. She wanted to turn the tables on him. "So she thinks you're a gigolo?"

He was just as quick. "So she thinks you have to pay to have a man want you?"

"Maybe she realizes I like to be in control," she said, staring down her nose at him.

The waitress returned and Lindsay quickly signed the charge slip, handed it to the waiting woman and slid out of the booth.

Gil joined her. "In control, huh?" he said under his breath. Then, as the waitress turned away, he pulled Lindsay against him and kissed her.

The warmth of his lips against hers melted something deep inside her. Before Lindsay could respond, as she realized with humiliation she would've done, he released her and said, "Thanks for the breakfast, darlin'."

Then he walked out of the café.

Gil called himself all kinds of a fool for giving in to temptation. First of all, because he might have lost his ride back to Oklahoma. Lindsay might be so mad at him she'd leave him standing in the snow outside the Roadrunner Café.

But the biggest reason he shouldn't have touched her was because it only made him hungrier to touch her again. To hold her as he had all through the night. What a shame to have wasted all that time sleeping.

She swept past him like a film star and unlocked the car.

He stood there waiting for her reaction.

"I'm leaving," she snapped. "If you're coming with me, you'd better shake a leg."

He didn't waste any time. As soon as he'd fastened his seat belt, she backed the car out of the parking space and headed for the interstate.

Six hours later, they'd exchanged few words. He figured she still hadn't forgiven him. But he'd watched her as she'd driven, noticing the exhaustion that was gradually claiming her.

"I offered to help with the driving. Want me to

take over now?'' he finally said, figuring she'd never ask for any help.

"Take over?'' she repeated stiffly, irritation still in her voice.

"Poor choice of words,'' he said immediately. "I meant, do you want me to spell you. You've done all the driving so far, and it's still another four or five hours 'til we get home.''

"I'm fine,'' she assured him, never looking his way. "There's a town coming up. Want to see if they have a fast-food place to get some lunch?''

They'd made one stop for fuel since breakfast and he was ready to eat, and stretch his legs. The small car was turning into a torture chamber. And not just because of lack of legroom. The woman was too close to him. He couldn't escape her scent, her warmth, the temptation of touching her.

"Yeah, that'd be good.''

He convinced her to go into a small café rather than hit a drive-through window. If she was determined to do all the driving, she needed a break now and then.

"I'm surprised we found something open on Thanksgiving Day,'' she said after they were seated.

A cheerful waitress greeted them. "We're open every day of the year, honey. We got regulars who wouldn't have any place to go. You two going home for the holidays?''

"Yes,'' Lindsay replied.

"That's nice. What can I get ya? We got the Thanksgiving Day special, turkey and all the trimmings.''

"That will be fine," Lindsay said with a tired smile.

"Me, too," Gil agreed. He was concentrating on Lindsay instead of the food. After the waitress left, he leaned forward. "How you feeling?"

"I'm fine." She didn't look at him.

"Will it help if I apologize?"

Her gaze collided with his before she looked away. "Apologize for what?"

"For kissing you at breakfast. I shouldn't have done that."

"Because it reminded you of your ex-wife, your marriage?"

He could hear the bitterness in her voice, which surprised him. But what surprised him even more was the fact that thoughts of his wife had never entered his head.

For the past two years, any woman he encountered had been compared to Amanda. And neither had come out smelling like a rose. He'd been filled with distaste.

Thoughts of Lindsay filled him with hunger. And no reminders of Amanda. "No. No, because I shouldn't have taken advantage of you."

Her tense shoulders sagged just a little and he was encouraged.

"I shouldn't have suggested you were a gigolo."

He smiled. "I've been called worse."

The waitress returned with two plates filled with steaming turkey and dressing and green beans. "I'll be right back with your coffee."

Lindsay stared at her plate, not moving.

"You okay?" Gil asked, concern filling him. Had she pushed herself too far? Was she getting sick?

She met his gaze briefly and he was dismayed to see tears in her eyes. Shaking her head, she picked up her fork.

"Lindsay? What's wrong? Did I say something I shouldn't have?" he asked, trying to think if he'd offended her in some way.

The waitress brought the coffee. "You folks need anything else right now?"

He hurriedly assured her they didn't.

"Well, save room for pie 'cause it comes with the meal. Besides, Joe makes the best pecan pie you've ever tasted."

When she'd left the table, a sob escaped Lindsay.

Gil shot out a hand and grabbed her wrist. "Lindsay, what's wrong?"

"Nothing! Nothing, I'm being silly."

"Tell me," he ordered, but his tone was gentle.

After a moment's hesitation, she burst out, "I thought I'd be home today, sharing turkey with my family."

Relief filled him as he released her wrist. "That's it? You're homesick?"

She gave a definite sniff and glared at him. "You needn't make it sound so stupid. I know—"

"Baby, I didn't mean—"

"Don't call me that!" she snapped, dabbing at her eyes with her napkin.

He hadn't even realized he'd used his pet name for his little sister. Damn. More carefully, he tried again. "Lindsay, I don't think it's stupid. But I was afraid you were getting sick, or something was really wrong.''

She didn't look at him, picking up her fork again and taking a bite of turkey. "Probably I'm just hungry.''

"I know I am," he assured her, taking a bite, too, and finding it surprisingly good.

But the hunger he was feeling wasn't for food.

And it wasn't likely he'd be able to satisfy it any time soon.

Chapter Five

Back on the road again, Lindsay seemed somewhat revived by their meal. But she'd still refused his second offer to do any driving. He figured she wouldn't relinquish the wheel all the way to Oklahoma, no matter how tired she became.

Hardheaded woman.

At least she'd forgiven him for the kiss. His gaze fastened onto her mouth, noting the generous bottom lip he'd tasted earlier. It had been wonderfully soft, inviting. In fact, he'd been surprised she hadn't hauled off and leveled him.

She must be too much a lady to brawl in public. Something else different from Amanda. She had enjoyed the attention public argument gave her. She considered herself a diva.

"Do you have a herd of cattle on your place?"

Gil looked at her in surprise. They hadn't bothered

with much friendly conversation during the drive. "Yeah, I've got a herd of Charolais."

"Oh. I thought you might be raising horses. There are several horse ranches around Apache."

"Yeah. And I am. That's what I'm really interested in, but we have a lot of acreage. I didn't see any point in letting it go to waste." And Rafe loved the breed. In fact, as a bonus last year, he'd given Rafe a number of heifers and free breeding rights to his bull. They'd branded Rafe's cattle and run them in with the main herd.

"What kind of horses?"

"Cutting horses." No showy breeds for him. Working horses, so vital to the operation of a ranch. He and Rafe worked together on training the animals. He'd even begun to build a reputation for the training of them.

Lindsay asked several more detailed questions, showing her knowledge of ranch life. Gil found himself relaxing, expanding on his hopes, his plans for the future.

"Hey," he said after going on for several minutes, "I'm probably boring you silly."

"No, I'm enjoying it. You remind me so much of my dad and brothers. They never think of anything else but ranching."

"And ordering around their little sister?"

"That, too," she agreed with a smile. "They've probably gotten a lot more done in the past year and a half since I've been gone."

"I bet they've gotten out of the habit of bossing you around and you'll find yourself with all kinds of freedom this visit." He couldn't imagine any man forgetting Lindsay Crawford, but maybe her brothers could.

She sighed. "I wish, but I think they were born being bossy, or they learned it at Daddy's knee."

"Aren't any of them married? That would take their attention off you."

"Only Logan. He moved to Texas a couple of years ago and married his boss. Abby is wonderful. She encouraged me to—to become my own woman."

"He married his boss? Didn't he find that, uh, awkward?" Gil couldn't imagine working for a woman *and* bedding her, too.

Lindsay grinned. "That's what my other brothers said. But Logan actually bought in as a partner. They're very happy."

Lindsay's brother's name struck a chord of memory. "Where in Texas?"

"Near Wichita Falls. Only a couple of hours from our place."

"I visited a place near there. There's a trainer, Jed Davis. I talked to him about training horses."

Lindsay beamed at him, and he caught his breath. Her radiance left him speechless.

"That's Abby's brother-in-law! Her younger sister Beth's husband. What a small world. Logan and Abby's home is just across the road."

"I guess it *is* a small world," he said, unable to come up with anything more original. Not when he was still basking in the warmth of her smile. Lordy, a man would do most anything to bring that look to her face again.

"Beth and Jed have a little boy three years old,

and Abby told me they're expecting again. And Abby's other sister, Melissa, and her husband, Rob, have a boy just a little younger. And Abby and Logan have a girl. You should see Logan with his daughter—she's got him wrapped around her little finger just like Abby does.'' She finished with a deep sigh of happiness.

"When I was there, Jed's son was a toddler."

"He's grown a bit. He has lots of children to play with when you include Rob and Melissa's seven children."

"Seven? She must've had triplets or something." He'd seen Beth. She wasn't very old. In fact, Jed had said something about his child bride, joking about doing whatever she wanted.

Lindsay chuckled, a sound that warmed Gil's blood. "No, not at all. Rob already had a daughter, Terri. She's fifteen now. And Melissa started a foster home for siblings. She was given two little girls, sisters, who were abandoned." Looking at Gil, she said, "You should see them, Gil. They're such precious little girls. And their parents just left them! How could anyone be so cruel?"

"I don't know, baby," he said softly, then hurriedly corrected himself. "I mean, Lindsay."

She pretended she hadn't heard his slip, but he knew she had by the sidelong glance she gave him.

"Anyway, they're darling. Then a neighbor and his wife were killed in a car crash. Melissa took in their three children so they wouldn't have to be separated and sent to different homes. And now they have one of their own."

"That's a lot of kids."

"Yeah," she agreed, but Gil could read the pleasure on her face. She wanted to be a mother. Some women seemed to have the nesting instinct. Others, like Amanda, never thought beyond themselves and should never have children. Not that she would have agreed to a child anyway, as he had learned to his own dismay. He cleared his throat. "You planning on a big family?"

She gave him another sidelong look. "Yes." Her chin rose, as if she thought he'd challenge her decision.

"In Chicago?"

Several minutes passed, and he wondered if he'd asked the wrong question.

Finally, she said, "That depends on my husband, and—and where my career takes me."

"What kind of career are we talking about, here? What do you do in Chicago?"

"I'm an assistant buyer at Bloomingdale's, in the housewares department."

"I figured they'd put you in fashion. You have the looks for it." Well, not quite. While she had a terrific figure, from a man's point of view, and curves in all the right places, she didn't have the reed-thin body of a model.

He was celebrating those curves, salivating over them, when he caught Lindsay's glare.

"Uh, what?"

"You think a woman can't look good *and* care about her house?"

"I didn't say that!" he protested at once. "I mean,

I thought you'd—you seem to know a lot about fashion.''

"How would you know?"

He shrugged his shoulders. "I saw you yesterday."

"I minored in retailing," she admitted, "concentrating in fashion, but the only opening they had at the time was housewares. And I wanted to get away from home."

No need to ask why. She'd made it clear her family was way too protective. So, in spite of being raised on a ranch, she was a city girl by choice. Like Amanda, who had come from a small Indiana town. She had headed to New York City as soon as she could, conveniently forgetting her roots.

And Lindsay would stay a city girl. Assistant buyers at Bloomingdale's wouldn't find any opportunities hanging on the trees on an Oklahoma ranch.

Abruptly, he asked a question that had been bothering him since yesterday. "Who gave you your ring?" Not that he was interested in any future with Lindsay Crawford, but it was a good idea to have all the facts.

She sent him a startled look. "My parents, for my twenty-first birthday. Why?"

"No reason. Just curious." Curious to know if some man had legitimate claims. Curious to know if she let men give her expensive presents. Curious to find out more about Miss Lindsay Crawford. For no reason.

Gil settled back in his car seat and told her he thought he'd take a nap. Before he tripped over any more land mines, or said something he shouldn't.

* * *

Lindsay looked at her watch. It was after six. They could stop for a meal, but they were only a couple of hours away. She knew her mother would have something waiting for them, and she was anxious to get home. But she wasn't sure she could keep going.

Her gaze shifted to the man beside her. He'd actually gone to sleep, his head pillowed against one of his hands on the window. She looked back to the road as he began to stir. Had he realized she was staring at him?

Shifting in his seat, he lifted his head and then rubbed his face. "Wow, I didn't think I'd go to sleep. How are you doing?"

"Feeling envious."

"Pull over and I'll give you the same opportunity."

She hadn't intended to let him drive, to leave him in control while she slept. But they'd shared more than twenty-four hours. And much to her surprise, she trusted him.

So she pulled over.

Only to find him staring at her, disbelief on his face. "You're actually going to let me drive?"

"Did you mean it when you—"

"Of course I did. But I didn't think you'd trust me."

She shrugged her shoulders. Better not tell him that letting him drive was nothing compared to sharing a bed with him. She'd prefer he think their closeness hadn't bothered her at all.

When she opened the door, after checking for oncoming traffic, she noticed the air was warmer than the last time she'd gotten out of the car. Not comfortable without a coat but a lot better than frozen Chicago.

She and Gil met at the back of the car. "You are alert, aren't you? Do you need some time to wake up?"

"Nope, I'm fine. I can't believe I slept. I haven't taken a nap in years." He circled around her to reach the driver's side.

When she got into the passenger's seat, she found it still warm from Gil's body. She shivered at the thought.

"You cold?" he asked, proving he'd been watching her. "My coat's in the back seat. Why don't you pull it over you?"

She hesitated. "I don't think I'll go to sleep."

"Maybe not, but you should get comfy. Use it as a pillow if you want."

She reached back for his coat, then fastened her seat belt. When she'd done that, Gil pulled out into traffic, handling her car as if he'd driven it forever.

She should've known he'd be a good driver. He seemed to do everything well. Snuggling down inside his coat, letting his scent surround her, her eyes drifted shut. They were tired from staring at the road. She'd just rest them for a few minutes.

Gil threw Lindsay a look. She was sleeping. Her beautiful face looked as angelic as a small child's when it was relaxed in sleep. And it also reminded him of this morning. He wished he'd been the first to awaken.

But he suspected the fact that he was asleep when

she awoke made it easier for her to accept his apology. Her immediate trust in him had made him feel pretty good. She had regressed during the day, but at least she had trusted him enough to drive.

He passed a sign showing twenty miles to Oklahoma City. From there, they only had another hour to go. He even knew how to reach her home. When he'd been slouched down in his seat, his eyes closed, he realized he'd met several of her brothers at one of the local rodeos.

Once he'd even gone to their ranch to look at a young colt they had for sale. He'd bought the youngster and the horse was turning into one of his favorite rides. That day he'd even met Caleb Crawford himself, Lindsay's father. A big, burly, jovial man, he'd welcomed Gil warmly, offered any help he needed with his new place.

Rafe knew the entire family. Said they were good people. If he'd told Rafe who he was driving back with, he probably would've been able to tell him even more details about the family.

He stamped down any desire to find out more about Lindsay. She was heading back to Chicago in a few days. If he was fortunate, he'd forget about her before she even left Oklahoma.

He sighed as he realized that wasn't a possibility. Having spent the night holding her against him, sharing all this time with her—kissing her—he'd be lucky if he'd forgotten her by *next* Thanksgiving.

Definitely he needed to develop a social life. Rafe had been telling him he was too young to spend all his time at the ranch, with only his manager for company.

He looked at Lindsay again. Too bad she'd be gone so quickly. He could've taken her to dinner a couple of times. Shown her his ranch. She knew enough about ranching to appreciate the work he'd done. To ask intelligent questions. She would make the perfect rancher's wife.

Except that she was a city girl. Besides, while he was glad she had shown some trust in him, he had to admit he didn't offer that quality often himself. He had naively placed his heart in Amanda's hands and had it thoroughly trampled. He had vowed never to be that foolish again.

No, it was a good thing she was leaving. That kept him from getting addicted to her presence.

She shifted in her seat, as if trying to find a more comfortable spot. With an eagerness that worried him, he reached out his right arm and pulled her head against his shoulder. With a sigh, she settled into him, a smile on her lips.

"Oh, baby," he muttered, drawing in her scent, feeling her soft hair brush his jaw. Yeah, it was a good thing she was leaving.

Gil turned down a dirt road that he was pretty sure led to the Crawford ranch. Now that they'd left the freeway with its bright lights, and even the farm-to-market road, the interior of the car was darker, more intimate.

Lindsay had shifted several times in her sleep. The last time, she'd turned more in to him and rested her hand across his stomach. Her touch burned into him, and left him both praying and fearing that it might slip just a little farther south.

He dropped his lips to her brow again. Several times he'd caressed her gently, needing to touch her somehow. He didn't think she'd object to such benign kisses. Of course, he wasn't going to test that theory by telling her. Nope, he wasn't an idiot.

But desire had been building inside him. For over an hour he'd held her against him, one hand on her and one on the steering wheel.

The ranch house came into view, a light flooding the area near it. The intimacy of the car was about to be invaded. He'd surrender Lindsay to her family and never see her again.

The pain that shot through him was jolting, unexpected. Okay, so he was attracted to the woman. A man would have to be made out of concrete not to respond to Lindsay's body, her warmth, her mind, her smile.

But he'd forget her. Of course he would.

He stopped the car near the front door, putting it in park. Before he cut the motor, he decided he deserved a little reward...and a goodbye.

Pulling Lindsay closer, he tipped her head up and covered her wonderful lips with his. A goodbye kiss. He felt her coming awake in his arms, but she didn't pull away. In fact, her arms slid up his chest to encircle his neck.

A jealous surge made him question who she thought she was kissing. Whoever it was had the right to be angry with him, but he didn't care. Nothing could make him call a halt to the wonderful exchange of passion that would keep him warm for many a night.

Until the car door opened and strong hands jerked Gil from the car and Lindsay's arms.

"Hey!" Gil protested.

He was spun around and just had time to notice his assailant had friends before a big fist collided with his chin.

"Daddy!" Lindsay shrieked, her voice piercing the pain that shot through Gil.

Great. He was being attacked by Lindsay's father. There went his intention of retaliating. Even if he wanted to, he couldn't hit an old man.

He shook his head to clear it, and the forms of four men became clear. The older man, Caleb Crawford, was preparing to hit him again.

"Hey, Dad, you've had your shot. It's our turn now," one of the men said.

So he was to become a punching bag for the Crawford clan? He didn't think so. He took hold of Caleb's hand, still clutching his shirt, and shoved it away.

"I—" he began, about to announce his intention to fight back, when Lindsay stopped him.

"If anyone touches him, you'll have to fight me next!" she insisted, her voice hot with rage. She shoved her way out of the car, past Gil, and stepped in front of him.

He put his hands on her shoulders to move her out of danger, but she whirled around to face him. "What are you doing?"

"I'm trying to get you out of firing range of these maniacs," he said with a growl.

She turned back around. "These maniacs are my family. They won't hit *me*."

"Not on the chin, young lady," Caleb assured her, his voice a deep burr, "but you may have trouble sitting down for a while."

Gil could feel her stiffen in shock as she took in her father's words.

"Mr. Crawford—" he began, unsure what to say. He'd figured Lindsay had exaggerated the behavior of the male members of her family, but now he wasn't so sure. If a kiss upset them this much, he'd hate to think what his fantasies would generate.

"We'll deal with you in a minute," the man snapped. "Lindsay, get in the house."

That the man expected immediate obedience was obvious to everyone. Lindsay, however, didn't move. Not exactly a surprise to Gil.

"No," she said firmly.

"Young lady, did you hear me? You get in the house right now. I don't want you seeing what's going to happen next."

"What's going to happen next, Dad, is I'm getting back in my car and heading back to Chicago, and taking Gil with me."

"But you just got here!"

"Yes, but there's no point in staying with the welcome you've given me."

Gil heard the hurt in her voice. The desire to comfort her, to wrap his arms around her and tell her—what? He didn't know what to say.

"Hell, girl, did you expect me to congratulate this bastard for seducing my little girl? For taking advantage of you? I told you to be careful up there in Chicago. You can't trust those city men!"

Lindsay proved she didn't need Gil's comfort. She slapped her hands on her hips and roared back at her father. "This city man lives in Apache! And all he did was kiss me! Since when is that a crime? Are you telling me you've attacked every woman my brothers have kissed? Because if you did I figure there wouldn't be any women left in the county!"

"Here, now, Lindsay, don't be yelling at me," Caleb ordered, but Gil could hear uneasiness in his voice.

"I'm only yelling because you are. When you're ready to speak in a reasonable tone of voice, so will I. But I won't be ordered around like a rag doll, and I won't let you beat up poor Gil."

Poor Gil? Gil didn't much appreciate that tag. "I can defend myself, Lindsay. I don't need your protection."

She whirled around again. "Don't you dare go all macho on me, Gil Daniels. This is ridiculous!"

"Gil? Gil Daniels, is that you?" one of the voices in the foursome asked.

Several others chimed in, and even Caleb stared at him. "The one who bought that colt?"

"Yeah, it's me," Gil acknowledged, but he kept his voice stern. He'd have a bruise tomorrow, which didn't put him in a forgiving mood.

"What are you doing with Lindsay? How'd she connect up with you?" Pete Crawford asked.

"Do you mind if we have this conversation after I put on my coat?" Gil asked. The wind was blowing right through him, and he noticed Lindsay was shivering.

"We'll go in the house, Gil," Lindsay said. "But there's no need for any conversation with these animals. You don't owe them any explanation." She took her coat as Gil handed it to her and shrugged into it.

"Listen here, little girl," Caleb said, anger still in his voice, "don't think you can bring your city ways back home. I don't know what you've been up to in Chicago, but back here, you'll abide by our rules."

"So kissing is against the rules?" she challenged, her chin up.

Gil couldn't hold back a grin. She was a fighter.

"No," her father snapped. "But sleeping with a man you're not married to sure is!"

Chapter Six

Lindsay thought of several responses to her father's statement. But she didn't give any of them. Instead, she took Gil's arm and started toward the house.

Her father and three of her brothers were on their heels, as if herding them. Only the back door opening and her mother's call of welcome kept her going. The urge to run, as she'd done when she left for Chicago, filled her. Nothing had changed. Nothing ever would.

Her mother's warm hug brought tears to her eyes, but she knew that warmth wouldn't solve her problems. "Mom, this is Gil Daniels. He drove down from Chicago with me."

Gil greeted her mother with perfect manners, but Lindsay recognized her mistake at once. Her mother thought she'd invited Gil home with her for the holidays.

"No, Mom," she said, before her mother could speak. "Gil isn't an unexpected guest. At least, not for long. He lives in Apache. He was visiting his sister in Chicago and got caught by the snowstorm and a canceled flight. He asked for a ride." She turned to glare at her father. "Though I suspect he'd prefer the snow to the kind of welcome he received here."

Her father glared back. "I won't apologize for trying to protect my daughter."

"Protect me from what? I'm twenty-five, Dad. If I want to kiss a man, I think I'm old enough."

"I'm not just talking about kissing. You slept together, didn't you?" The level of his accusation rose as he spoke, until he finished with a roar.

"No!" Lindsay shouted back.

"Yes," Gil said calmly.

Lindsay spun around to stare at Gil. "What did you say?"

"You know what I said. I have no intention of lying to your father."

She gasped. Her gaze flickered to her father's enraged features and then back to Gil. "Nothing happened!"

"I know. But we did sleep together."

"But we didn't have sex, you idiot!" She was almost as mad at Gil as she was at her father. His claim of honesty had just made things worse.

"Maybe you'd better explain, Daniels," Caleb Crawford said forcefully.

"Sure, I'll—"

"You'll do no such thing!" Lindsay snapped. She was old enough not to be interrogated about her personal behavior. She decided she should begin as she meant to go on.

"Lindsay, darling, have you and Gil eaten anything? I have some turkey saved for you." Her mother took her arm to urge her toward the kitchen.

"Mom, I'm not going to abandon Gil to them. He's already been slugged once. They might—"

With a stern look in her husband's direction, Carol said, "Your father isn't going to do any more hitting tonight. Right, Caleb? Or your brothers, Lindsay. Now come help me fix a couple of plates for you and Gil."

Before she conceded to her mother's orders, she looked at Gil one more time. "Don't say a word." Then she headed for the kitchen.

Gil knew better than to obey Lindsay's order. He could sympathize with Caleb Crawford, though he didn't appreciate being the recipient of all that anger.

"Look, Mr. Crawford, if you'll let me explain—"

"Go ahead. But be prepared for the consequences," the older man said with a growl.

"Lindsay and my sister are neighbors in Chicago. When my flight got canceled, I offered to pay the expenses and help with the driving if Lindsay would give me a ride home. We got caught in the blizzard. When she finally agreed to stop for the night, the only motel within our reach had one room left. With one bed. We shared the bed, but we didn't have sex."

Caleb stared at him, as if weighing his tale for its truthfulness. Gil had said his piece. He stood there in silence, awaiting the man's decision.

He'd told an abbreviated version of the past twenty-four-plus hours. There was no mention of the sexual hunger his companion had inspired. Or the two kisses they'd shared.

Caleb Crawford didn't deserve that much honesty.

"You sure that's the truth, Daniels?" Caleb asked.

Gil stiffened. He wasn't used to his honesty being questioned. "Yes, Mr. Crawford. That's the truth."

The kitchen door swung open and Lindsay and her mother entered.

Mrs. Crawford smiled at Gil. "Come here to the table, Gil. You must be starved. Caleb, boys, do you want coffee? I've got some pie left, too. Everyone come sit down."

Pete, one of the brothers Gil had met before, stepped closer to his father. "If Gil says that's the truth, Dad, you can trust him. His word is good."

Caleb nodded and moved toward the table.

Just as Gil let himself relax, with a nod of gratitude toward Pete, Lindsay exploded.

"So that's it? You accept a stranger's word, but your own daughter's isn't good enough, Dad? What did he tell you? Did he reveal something that convinced you to believe him, but not me? Or am I just a second-class citizen, like I've always been?"

Even her mother protested those harsh words. "Lindsay!"

"Don't you ever get tired of it, Mom?" she asked, whirling to stare at the woman behind her. "They want you to cook and clean for them, but you get no say in anything!"

"That's not true, dear," her mother said calmly.

"It certainly is not!" Caleb denied, his face turning red again.

Gil decided it was time to exit this family confrontation. "Pete, if I can use the phone, I'll get my ranch manager to come get me."

Pete, and the other two young men bearing a striking resemblance to him, looked uneasily at his parents and sister. "Uh, why don't I give you a ride? It'll be faster and I bet you're tired."

"Sure, that'd be great," he agreed. He didn't have any place in the middle of Lindsay's family argument.

She must have thought differently. In the angry glare she cast his way, he also saw hurt, as if she thought he was abandoning her without offering her any help. "Lindsay—" he began.

But she didn't wait. Without saying a word, she walked from the room and slammed the door behind her.

Gil wanted to chase her, to pull her into his arms and assure her he hadn't meant to disappoint her. But he had no right—and no reason—to do so. After all, they were acquaintances, nothing more. True, they'd spent some trying hours together, but there was no future for them. He was staying in Oklahoma. She was returning to Chicago.

Everyone seemed frozen in shock. He cleared his throat. "If that offer still stands, Pete, I'd appreciate a lift."

Pete shook off his immobility. "Sure thing. You got stuff in Lindsay's car?"

"Yeah, but I think the keys are still in the ignition. I can get them on my way to your truck."

"But don't you want to eat, Gil?" Carol asked. "I have the food ready."

"Thank you, Mrs. Crawford, but I'll grab something at home. Besides, I imagine Lindsay will be glad to see the last of me. She's—she's pretty hurt by everything.'' It wasn't his place to rebuke Lindsay's family, but she hadn't received much of a welcome from these people.

Caleb cleared his throat. "No hard feelings, Daniels? You know how it is, with daughters. You try to protect them—''

"But finally you have to let them grow up.'' With a nod, he walked to the door. If he stayed much longer, he might explain to Caleb Crawford what a mistake he was making with his only daughter.

Since he was so experienced with children. The father of so many daughters. Yeah, he'd best get away while he could.

Lindsay woke early the next morning in her old room. The familiarity of it was soothing, until the previous night's events filled her head.

She regretted the way she'd handled everything and everyone last night. She'd fallen right back into the pattern of challenging her father at every turn.

And he, of course, had fought back.

"But he started it,'' she muttered to herself. Hearing those childish words only confirmed her condemnation of her behavior. She'd promised herself that this time she'd remain calm. Her father might not have changed, but she'd been sure *she* had.

Her biggest humiliation, and disappointment, she silently confessed to herself, was behaving so poorly in front of Gil. He hadn't been too impressed with her before, telling her she reminded him of his ex-wife. He made it clear that wasn't a compliment.

Now he could add immature and spoiled to her resume.

She'd never see him again.

Tears filled her eyes at the thought. They hadn't even had a full two days together. He shouldn't mean anything to her.

But he did.

A soft knock on her door preceded it opening. Her mother said, "Are you awake, darling? That nice Gil Daniels is on the phone."

Gil? Calling her? She checked her watch even as she sat up. It was almost eight-thirty. "Yes, I'm awake. I'm sorry I slept so late, Mom."

"That's all right, dear. You're a city girl, after all. You don't have to conform to our country ways." Her mother's smile was warm, but her words hurt.

"City people don't get to sleep late, Mom. I had to be at the store by eight every day." She knew eight didn't sound early when her brothers and father ate breakfast at six during the spring and summer, but she usually got up at six-thirty.

Grabbing her robe off the end of the bed, she pulled it on as she headed for the door. She had to go to the kitchen to talk to Gil.

She was breathless when she reached the phone. Drawing a deep breath, in an effort to sound calm and relaxed, she said, "Hello?"

"Lindsay, it's Gil. I wanted to call and thank you again for giving me a ride home."

His formal words hadn't been what she wanted to hear. "I appreciated the help in driving."

Silence.

So all he had to say was a thank-you? Was that

all they had to talk about? Truthfully, she couldn't think of anything to say, either, but she didn't want to hang up.

Finally, his voice softened to an intimate level and he asked, "Are you all right?"

Lindsay leaned against the wall, warmth filling her as she heard the concern in his voice. "Yes. Are you? Did you have a bruise this morning?"

"A little one. No big deal. Did you work things out with your dad?"

She couldn't hold back the way her body stiffened, her jaw squared. "No."

More silence.

"Look, I know you don't have much time here, and if you want to spend it all with your family, I'll understand, but I thought you might like to see my ranch. You seemed interested when I talked about it and..."

"I'd love to. When should I come?"

"I'll come get you."

"No, I can drive myself. This morning? I mean, when—"

"This morning would be great. I'd like you to meet Rafe, too, my manager. He knows your family."

Her mother slid a mug of coffee on the cabinet beside her and she smiled her thanks.

"I'd love to meet him. Can you give me directions?"

He did so, then added, "And plan on staying for lunch, if you'd like. I'm not a great cook, but we can fix ham sandwiches, if that'll do."

"It'll do fine. I'll see you in about an hour." She

hung up the phone and turned to face her mother. "Gil invited me to come see his ranch today."

"How nice. Is it an hour away?"

"No, less than half an hour. But I have to have breakfast and shower. I don't want to go looking like a slob," she assured her mother. She took a sip of coffee and then headed for the pantry. Her mother had her favorite cereal in its usual place and she began pouring some into a bowl.

"Could you work in a few minutes to speak to your father?" her mother asked softly, pouring herself another cup of coffee and sitting at the table.

Lindsay froze. Then she reminded herself of her game plan. Calm strength. That hadn't been her reaction last night. But with rest and food, she'd be stronger. "Of course. Is he in the barn?" Even as she asked, she crossed the room and sat down across from her mother with her cereal.

"Yes, he is. He feels badly about last night. You see, he hated not talking to you when you called yesterday morning. So he called the motel to speak with you, but the clerk told him you and your, um, man, had just left. I'm afraid he leapt to conclusions. And they stewed in him all day long." She hastily held up her hand when Lindsay opened her mouth to protest. "I'm not defending his behavior, dear, just explaining."

Calm strength. Lindsay chanted those words in her head like a mantra. "I understand, Mom," she finally said, after drawing a deep breath, "but a little faith in my judgment would be nice."

"Yes, dear, but you're his only daughter." Her

mother's tolerant smile didn't encourage Lindsay's serenity.

"He would never question the boys' behavior."

"You'll have to ask your brothers about that," she said with a chuckle. "Most of those confrontations occurred in the barn, so you didn't see them."

"Then how do you know about them?" Lindsay asked.

"Your father told me. Most of *our discussions* occurred in the bedroom, so you weren't privy to them, either," her mother chided.

Lindsay ducked her head. She wasn't convinced, but she owed her mother an apology. "I'm sorry I said the things I did last night."

"And I'm sorry your welcome wasn't all it should've been. We've all missed you so much. Last year, you were hardly here long enough to open presents."

Lindsay managed to keep the tears at bay and reached out to take her mother's hand. She'd missed them desperately, too. Until last night.

"But we talk on the phone every week," she reminded her mother.

"Yes, but that's not the same as being together. Your father began to think you'd never come home again."

"After last night—" Lindsay began, then remembered her plan. With a deep breath, she started over. "I've missed everyone, too."

"Good. Tell your father that."

The sound of the back door opening brought her mother to her feet. "That will be Mrs. Brown. I meant to make a list for her before I go to town. I've got a meeting at the library at ten o'clock. Do you need anything from town?''

''No, thanks, Mom. I'll have lunch at Gil's and be back later this afternoon.''

Her mother paused on her way out of the kitchen. ''Are you interested in Gil?''

''His sister and I are good friends.'' That didn't exactly answer her mother's question, but it was the only answer Lindsay had for her.

She couldn't be interested in Gil. There was no future there. The man had no intention of marrying or having a family. And she reminded him of his ex-wife.

And then there was the evaporation of her own plans.

She'd be heading back to Chicago tomorrow.

With a sigh, she finished her cereal, then greeted Mrs. Brown, her mother's longtime housekeeper, as she entered the kitchen. She had worked for her mother since Lindsay was four. She was a second mother to Lindsay and commiserated often with the inequality of the sexes on the Crawford ranch.

After a shower and the donning of comfortable jeans and shirt, topped with a jean jacket, Lindsay straightened her shoulders, drew a deep breath, and headed for the barn.

''Dad?'' she called as she walked into the big structure's shadowy depths. The smell of hay and animals was a scent she was well familiar with. It made her feel at home almost as much as her mother's warm, sunny kitchen.

''Lindsay?'' her father called seconds before he

emerged from the tack room in the back. "That you?"

"Yes, Dad." For the first time, she realized her father felt awkward about this meeting, unsure of what to say. That realization made it easier for her to step forward and hug his neck. His arms tightened around her.

"I'm sorry about last night, Dad."

"Oh, sweetheart, I am, too," he said in a rush. "I was just so worried about you."

"I'm fine, Dad." She wanted to argue his lack of faith. She wanted to tell him she'd grown up. She could take care of herself. But she'd promised herself she'd remain calm. Steady. Mature. "I wanted to tell you I'm going over to see Gil's ranch. He's invited me for lunch. So I'll see you this evening."

"The whole day? But I wanted to show you— Well, that's fine. I heard he has a nice operation."

"Maybe you can show me some things in the morning, before I leave."

"You're leaving that soon? I hoped you'd stay a few days." The dismay in her father's voice was a solace to her aches.

"Having to drive cut my time short. I'm supposed to be back at work on Monday morning," she explained.

"I don't know why you don't quit that job and come home. I could use your help here, pay you a salary."

His dismissal of her job, her work, hurt. But she reminded herself again of her plan. "I like my job, Daddy. I'll try to plan a longer stay next time."

To her surprise, her response had the desired effect. He pulled her close for another hug and agreed that that would be good. Then he warned her to be careful on her drive to Gil's, asked if she knew how to get there. She was tempted to tell him that she'd decided to drive around in circles until she happened upon Gil's ranch. But she refrained.

"Gil gave me directions."

"Oh, great. He's a good man. Couldn't do better."

Uh-oh. She knew what those words meant. "Daddy, Gil isn't interested in me. Don't start getting ideas."

"He looked pretty interested last night. And he invited you over today." His chin raised and he challenged her with his gaze.

It suddenly struck her that she might be looking into a mirror. When someone challenged her opinion, she came out of her corner fighting. Never so much as when the challenger was one of her family.

This time she backed away. "I'll see you this afternoon." Giving him a kiss on the cheek, she hurried from the barn.

"You keep staring at that road, it's going to disappear on you," Rafe drawled from behind Gil.

He spun around. "What are you talking about? I was just checking."

"Yep. Like you've been doing for the past hour."

Gil thought about arguing with his manager. But he only spoke the truth. After Lindsay accepted his invitation, Gil had hurriedly straightened up the kitchen, made his bed and headed for the barn. Since then, he'd worn out a path to the barn door to watch for Lindsay.

"She should be here soon, unless she got lost."

"Not likely. This place is easy to find. I can't wait to meet her. She's the first lady you've shown any interest in since you moved here."

"Don't be ridiculous! I'm not interested in Lindsay Crawford. I'm simply thanking her for giving me a ride. It's only polite."

"Uh-huh. Just good manners." Rafe grinned. "Your granny would've been proud."

Rafe, in his fifties now, had worked for Gil's grandmother most of his life. Gil had met him his first summer spent with his grandmother twenty years ago. Gil was used to his teasing.

"Okay, so she's good-looking. It doesn't matter. She's a city girl now, and she's heading back for Chicago right away. But I thought you'd enjoy a little female company before she left."

"So you were only thinking of me?" Rafe asked, still grinning.

Gil was about to answer him when he heard a car. He spun around and headed for the barn door, completely forgetting the conversation he'd been having.

Rafe leaned against the rake he'd been wielding and waited to see what happened next. He knew about last night. Gil had still been upset when he'd reached the ranch.

For two years, Rafe had worried about Gil. He'd come home from New York a bitter, reserved man. He'd remained on the ranch, avoiding most men and all women. For the first time in two years, he was eager to see a female.

Rafe couldn't wait to meet her.

Chapter Seven

Lindsay took note of the excellent condition of Gil's property. The fences were well strung, made from the latest material. His pastures were in excellent shape, still providing good feed for his cattle even this late in the year. The gravel drive that led to the ranch buildings was well maintained.

Having grown up on a ranch, she knew how much effort was required for those results, even if she hadn't been allowed to participate in it on her family's ranch.

The house caught her eye as she pulled to a stop. A large Victorian-style home, it had a covered porch running around three sides of it. She could imagine sitting there in the evening, rocking, discussing the day's events, Gil telling her— No, she didn't mean Gil but some fictitious husband. No one she knew.

Movement caught her attention and she saw Gil emerge from the barn and head toward her car. Excitement zipped through her as she got out. By the time she'd closed her door, he was there, his gaze focused on her lips.

He's going to kiss me! That thought left her breathless, eager, leaning toward him. Then he stuck out his hand.

She stared at it.

"Lindsay? I wanted to welcome you to my place."

Her cheeks flushed as she prayed he couldn't read her mind. She shook his hand and stepped back, bumping into her car. "Yes, thank you, it's so nice of you to invite me."

He reached out to stabilize her. "Don't trip. We don't want to start our day with an injury. Glad you wore jeans. I started to call back and warn you, because I'm hoping you're up to a little ride. But I decided to take a chance."

She knew he'd been testing her. She could just as easily have worn a skirt. If she had, he would've labeled her a city girl, through and through. She didn't like taking blind tests.

"I hoped we would do some riding," she said calmly, but the excitement she'd felt dimmed a little.

"Come meet Rafe."

He took her arm to guide her to the barn. His touch today set off the alarms as much as it had during their trip. It made her want more. Not a good thing.

"Is he in the barn, working? That's where Dad was, too."

"You spoke to your father this morning?"

He sounded surprised that she could do the mature thing. Of course, she hadn't shown much maturity last night, but his attitude still irritated her. "Yes, of course. We both apologized for our behavior. I'm afraid I lost control with the long trip and—and being hungry. I wasn't at my best."

"None of us were. I hope you ate some dinner before you went to bed. Rafe made me a big sandwich and we shared a pot of coffee while I caught up on everything."

So, he'd had a warm welcome. The kind she hadn't been offered. Good for him. That made Rafe a special man. She couldn't wait to meet him.

Since they were entering the barn, she didn't have to tell Gil that she'd gone to bed without eating or talking to anyone after their fight. In fact, she'd cried herself to sleep.

But this morning she'd been calm, mature, reasonable. If only she could erase last night and do it over.

An older man stepped forward from the shadows of the barn and offered a warm greeting. His face bore the traces of his mixed heritage, part Mexican-American and she suspected part Indian, but all cowboy.

After a brief chat, one she enjoyed because she was comfortable with cowboys, Gil led her to two horses waiting in a nearby corral, already saddled.

"I guess it is a good thing I wore jeans," she said with a shrug of her shoulders.

"We could take the truck, if you prefer, but—"

"No! I wasn't complaining. I miss riding. Sometimes in Chicago I go to a stable and hire a horse for an hour, but it's not the same."

"I know," Gil agreed with a grin. "I used to do the same thing in Central Park."

That shared understanding set the tone for their ride, and Lindsay loved every moment of it. When they returned to the barn several hours later, she was happier than she'd been in several years. Or maybe forever.

"I'm starved," Gil assured her as they unsaddled their mounts. "I'll take care of your ride in a minute, baby, I mean, Lindsay. You don't have to—"

"We'll get to eat that much sooner if I help," she said calmly. She wasn't about to be treated like a sissy, a dude, a doll who sat on a shelf.

"Fair enough," he agreed with a grin.

When they started for the house, he surprised her by taking her hand in his. After several hours of leisurely riding, watching his strong body control the large animal beneath him, Lindsay was already aware of him. When he touched her, shivers coursed through her body.

"You cold? It hasn't warmed up much, has it?"

"No, but it's a lot warmer than Chicago," she assured him, hoping he wouldn't realize the cause for her reaction.

He tucked her hand, encased in his, in his jacket pocket. "Rafe will have the kitchen warm and cozy. He promised to start making the sandwiches about noon."

"Is he the only worker you have?" she asked. They hadn't covered the entire ranch in the ride, but she hadn't seen anyone else.

"Nope. I cut back in winter, but there are two other hands. They're riding fence today on the north side."

They approached the house that had caught her

eye earlier. His barn was brand-new, with all the latest equipment. His ranch was up-to-date in every way. But he'd kept the charming old house.

"I'm glad you didn't tear the house down and rebuild," she said softly, her gaze tracing the ornate trim of the porch.

"You like it?"

"Oh, yes, it's wonderful. I can't wait to see inside."

She turned an eager smile on him but was puzzled by the way he avoided her gaze.

"It's just a house," he muttered.

They stepped up on the porch and he reached for the door, pulling it open and waving her inside.

She understood his reaction as soon as she entered. The outside of the house had been maintained and painted recently, its white sides sparkling in the winter sunshine. Inside, the walls were dingy, the floor uneven and stained, the equipment original to the house when it had been built almost a century ago.

She stood still, shocked by the neglect in the midst of the ranch's perfection.

"How was the ride?" Rafe asked from the kitchen counter where he was making sandwiches.

Lindsay stared at him, still trying to recover from the contrast of what she'd seen. "Uh, fine. Very enjoyable."

"I told you it was just a house," Gil muttered, crossing to the sink and washing his hands. "There's a bath just down the hall if you want to clean up."

She immediately excused herself, grateful for an opportunity to pull herself together.

* * *

"I told you you should fix this place up," Rafe muttered. "Didn't you prepare her? She looked kind of shocked."

Gil dried his hands. "She said she liked the house. She was glad I left it the way it was."

"Was that before or after she came inside?"

Not wanting to answer that question, Gil asked, "Are the sandwiches ready?"

"Yeah. She'll be as impressed with our cooking as she is with our decoratin'."

Gil ignored Rafe's dig. He'd made a conscious decision when he'd bought the ranch. While he poured any money necessary into the land, buying all the latest equipment, hiring good men to help him and Rafe, buying the start of his herd, horses that he thought would be good cutters, he'd spent nothing on the house.

At first, Rafe had assumed Gil had put off work on the house because of all the outside stuff they had to do. When he suggested some changes as winter approached that first year, Rafe had been shocked to discover Gil had no intention of making improvements in the old home. He still remembered the discussion they had over it.

"But, Gil, this place is drafty. And the hot water isn't very reliable. Cold showers in winter are tough!"

"You getting soft in your old age, Rafe?"

Rafe had stared at him. "I don't think it's being soft to want to avoid being a Popsicle."

"I like things the way they are."

A frown settled on Rafe's face. "Have we ruined you, boy? Are you broke?"

"No! No, I'm not broke, but I'm not fixing up the house. I don't want a showplace, something the neighbors can ooh and aah over. This is a working ranch."

And the subject had been closed.

He felt a little guilty now as he realized he could've made life easier for Rafe the past couple of years. His old friend had been patient with his stubbornness.

But after his final break with Amanda, he'd been furious with women, with pretension, with big cities, with everything but the basics of life. So Rafe had suffered.

Lindsay's entrance put an end to his thoughts. "Hungry?" he asked.

"Yes. A morning ride always sharpens my appetite," she said with a laugh that invaded Gil's dark thoughts and made him smile in return.

"Good. Rafe said everything's ready."

She smiled at his friend, and Gil was amazed to feel a surge of jealousy. No, that couldn't be! He didn't want a woman in his life.

A few minutes later, when their hunger had been satisfied, Rafe leaned back in his chair. "Gil said you like the house."

"It's a beautiful old place," she agreed, still smiling.

Gil was satisfied with her response…until she continued.

"Of course, it needs an incredible amount of work inside, but it would be worth the effort. It's the most beautiful example of Victorian architecture I've ever seen. Why, if you redid it, it would be an even bigger draw than the horses you're training. People love to see these old homes.''

"No!" Gil protested, unable to hold back the distaste building in him.

She leaned toward him. "I don't mean you have to decorate with doilies and fine china," she assured him with a laugh. "You're afraid it would be too feminine for you two tough cowboys, aren't you?" She laughed. "I promise it doesn't have to be. Why, even a good cleaning would make a big difference. And you'd want to update the plumbing and the electricity, of course and—"

"I don't want to do any of that," Gil said firmly.

"You're right," she said.

He sat back with a sigh.

"That would be pretty expensive. You could start off slowly with wallpaper, new paint, polish, and do a lot of the work yourself until you have more money available, but—"

This time Gil didn't leave any doubt of his response. He leapt to his feet and roared, "No! Nada, nothing! I'm not doing anything to this house. It's fine as it is and I'll thank you to take your ideas and your *fashion sense* out of my house!"

As silence fell, his gaze traveled from Lindsay's shocked face to Rafe's weary stare and back to Lindsay again. "I didn't mean—" he began, realizing he'd overreacted. But that realization had come too late.

Lindsay was already on her feet. But she didn't stalk out of the room, slamming the door behind her, as she had last night. Instead she looked at Rafe.

"Thank you so much for the lovely lunch, Rafe."

Then she walked out, without a word to Gil.

Once she was behind the wheel, with the windows tightly closed, Lindsay shared her opinion of the male race with the steering wheel, the radio and the empty seat beside her.

"Men! They are absolutely insane. And so sure they're always right. That had to be about his wife. Every time the word fashion comes up, he's talking about her!" she fumed. Then she added, "And me."

With a sigh she told herself what she'd already known. There was no future for her here. She may have hoped everything would have changed, that she could return to the life she loved, but she couldn't. How would she earn any money? And how could she bear her brothers' supervision? Her father was bad enough but at least he was her father. *They* had no right.

Worst of all, how could she live near Gil and not want to be with him? It may have only been two days, but those hours spent together had proven an attraction that could easily develop into something more.

But then she'd be married to someone just like her brothers.

On impulse, she took the long way home, reluctant to return to the ranch and the questions her family would ask. Questions she couldn't answer.

So she drove through Lawton, a larger town than Duncan or Apache that formed a triangle with them. When she passed slowly down one of the main streets, she caught the name of a dress shop and suddenly pulled into a nearby parking place.

Oklahoma Chic. Some people would call that an oxymoron, Lindsay thought with a smile. Probably one of those people would be Gil's ex-wife. But her mother had written her about Kelly Hampton opening a dress shop in Lawton.

She studied the windows of the shop critically. They were attractive, but she thought Kelly could do more with them. When she went in, the shop was almost empty. Which made it easy to surprise her old friend with a hug.

An hour later, Lindsay was feeling much better. Kelly respected her opinion and asked for advice after they'd talked over old times. She saw a lot of possibilities in the shop, but many of her suggestions would cost money.

"I know the old adage that you have to spend money to make money," Kelly said tiredly, "but when you don't have any, it doesn't much matter."

"Things are that bad?"

"Well, I had a lot of bills after Dave's death, and, while I was pregnant with Andrew, I was sick a lot. By the time he was born and I got back on my feet, I was in real trouble. The store kind of hit bottom then. I'm building it back up slowly, but I don't have any extra money to reinvest."

"I'm sorry, Kel. I think you have a great location. I'm sure you'll make it. It will just take a little longer." She gave her friend an encouraging smile.

They'd been best friends since the first grade, in spite of their different backgrounds. Lindsay came from a rich ranching family, one of six children, and Kelly came from a family made up of only her and her mother. Her mother supported them by working two shifts a day at the local diner in Duncan.

"Sure, we'll make it," Kelly said brightly. "Will you have time to come see Andrew?"

"Are you busy this evening?" Lindsay asked. "I know it's Friday night, but I'm going to have to leave tomorrow around noon."

"Friday night is no different from any other night, Lindsay, when you have a two-year-old," Kelly assured her with a wry grin.

"Okay. How about I pick up some pizza and meet you at your house?"

"That'd be great unless you're expecting it to be clean."

Lindsay assured her friend she'd be insulted if Kelly cleaned for her. Then she refused Kelly's offer to pay for half the pizza and said goodbye.

When she was back in her car, Lindsay reminded herself that, compared to Kelly, she had no problems. Maybe her brothers bossed her around. Maybe her father watched her like a hawk. But they loved her.

Maybe she wanted to come home and didn't feel she could. But she had a good job and a nice place to live.

Maybe she wanted Gil to— But she'd survive.

"Lindsay, is that you?" her mother called as she came into the house.

"Yes, Mom," she replied and moved into the kitchen, the gathering room in their house.

"I've been worried."

"I told you I'd be back this afternoon." She checked her watch. It wasn't even three yet.

"But Gil said you left there about one o'clock," Carol said, a questioning look in her eyes.

"Gil? He called?" She immediately shut down the flutter of her heart at hearing that news. "Why?"

"He didn't explain, dear. But it seemed awfully important that he talk to you. So I invited him to dinner." Her mother smiled at her, as if sure she'd be pleased.

"Really. And did he accept?"

"Of course, dear. He said he'd be here at six. I'm fixing roast beef, steamed vegetables, creamed potatoes and an apple pie." With a wink, she added, "Mrs. Brown made the pie earlier. I had to fight the boys to save it for tonight."

"I'm sure you did. I guess the guys won't be here for dinner, since it's Friday night."

"Only Mike is going out. He's meeting some of his friends from law school. But Joe, Pete and Rick will be here. They were all pleased to hear Gil is coming. They seem to approve—I mean, like him."

"Good for them. I hope they enjoy themselves." Lindsay kept moving through the kitchen, trying to hold on to her temper. Her mother was arranging her social life now without even checking with her.

"I hope we all enjoy ourselves," Carol said, a puzzled look on her face.

"I know I will, Mom, because I've already made plans."

She was almost out the door before her mother ordered her to halt.

She paused, her hand on the door, and looked over her shoulder. "Yes?"

"What do you mean you've made other plans? Gil

specifically is coming to see you. Of course you'll be here.''

Calm strength, Lindsay reminded herself. "Mom, Dad has always been the worst about running my life, but you've made arrangements for me before without asking. I've made plans with Kelly, and I won't be home for dinner. Had you asked me before you invited Gil, I would've told you. Sorry.''

"But—but what am I going to tell Gil?''

"Tell him you have apple pie. In fact, you probably should call and invite Rafe, too. I don't think either of them do much cooking. I'm sure he'd appreciate dinner, too. You'll like him.''

"Lindsay, I can't believe you'd be so rude. Please call Gil and tell him you won't be here.''

"No, Mom. I didn't invite him. And I don't want to talk to him.'' She attempted to make her escape again, but this time she was halted by her father's entry just as her mother offered another protest.

"What's wrong with Lindsay?'' Caleb boomed, his voice filling the kitchen.

"Nothing's wrong with Lindsay,'' Lindsay said calmly, smiling at her father. "I'm just going up to my room.''

"Have a good time at Gil's? Nice operation?''

"Wonderful. You should go visit him.'' She kept her smile in place and turned again to leave.

"I should? You telling me something, little girl? Should I ask him about his prospects tonight?''

Calm strength flew out the window. "Daddy! Don't you dare!'' she snapped as she whirled around.

Her big, strong father looked totally bewildered, turning to his wife for help. "What did I say?''

Lindsay charged across the kitchen. "There is nothing between me and Gil. Do you hear me? Absolutely nothing! The man has no intention of ever marrying again, and even if he did, I wouldn't have anything to do with him!" She almost added *because he reminds me of you,* but calm strength knocked some sense into her before she did.

"She's not going to be here for dinner," Carol said softly, her gaze on Lindsay.

"Mom!" Lindsay protested. She knew she wouldn't escape until her father gave her the third degree.

"What? The man's coming to see you and you're not going to be here? Now, little girl, that's no way—"

"I already have plans, Dad. I didn't know he was coming. Mom shouldn't have invited him on my behalf without checking with me first." She got those words out calmly, but her body was as tight as a new barbed wire fence, stretched between two poles.

"Couldn't you cancel your plans?" her father asked.

"No, I can't."

Then she finally made her escape from the kitchen.

Chapter Eight

Gil knocked off work a little early to shower and shave before he left for the Crawfords' for dinner. The blinking light on the answering machine stopped him.

Had Lindsay called to say the invitation was canceled? He wouldn't blame her. He'd been unforgivably rude today at lunch. As Rafe had told him.

Finally, he pushed the play button, holding his breath. Instead of Lindsay, it was Carol, her mother. "I thought I'd extend the dinner invitation to include Rafe. We'd love to have him join us also. No need to let me know. There'll be plenty of food."

Gil knew Rafe would enjoy an evening out. As hard as Rafe worked for him, Gil certainly wouldn't deny him dinner with friends. But he didn't want any more lectures. He knew his behavior had been unacceptable.

With a sigh, he went back out to the barn. "Rafe? You in here?"

Rafe's head popped up from the last stall. "Yeah, I was just checking on Sugarbaby."

"How's she doing?"

"Fine. I think we've got another week or two before she drops. Anything wrong?"

"Nope, but Mrs. Crawford left a message inviting you for dinner, too, if you want to come."

Rafe's eyes brightened. "Hey, I'd like that. Dinner neither you nor me cooked." He paused, then asked, "You don't mind?"

"Of course not. Why would I?"

"Well, I don't want to interfere with your courting Lindsay."

Gil drew a deep breath, knowing his face was turning beet red as he held back his temper. "I told you before, I'm not courting anyone! I was just being neighborly."

"Oh, yeah. Well, then, I'd like to eat with the Crawfords. They're nice people."

An hour later, they were on their way to the Double C ranch.

"You gonna apologize to Lindsay?" Rafe asked after saying nothing for most of the ride.

"Of course."

"Good."

"That's it? No advice on exactly what to say?" Gil growled.

"Nope. I don't like to interfere."

That blatant lie made Gil laugh. "Oh, yeah. I forgot."

"Here, now, boy. You know—"

"I know, Rafe. You're family, even if we're not really related. You can say whatever you want. You know I couldn't manage without you."

Rafe's cheeks darkened. "You're the boss," he protested.

"Yeah," Gil said with another chuckle. Then, his voice serious, he said, "I've been doing some thinking about family, since I got home."

Rafe stared at him. "Why?"

With a shrug, Gil said, "Lindsay has some problems with her family. I dismissed them at first, but the way they greeted her the other night...well, I began to understand a little more."

"They're good people," Rafe said stubbornly.

"Yeah, they are, but they don't make her feel good about herself."

"What are you? Some damn psychologist?"

"No, Rafe, but when I got home, you had food ready. You made me feel welcome. You asked about my trip, about Kathy. You made sure I was comfortable."

"You make me sound like the Beaver's mom," Rafe said in disgust.

Gil laughed again. "Yeah. But Lindsay's father yelled at her. He hadn't seen her in almost a year."

"I bet her mom didn't yell at her."

"No, and she hugged her, said how good it was to see her. But she didn't stop her husband from showing his anger."

"What was he angry about?"

Uh-oh. Gil hadn't intended to mention that fact. "Uh, he'd found out that—that Lindsay and I stopped for the night."

"He thought you'd driven straight through?" Rafe shook his head. "Why would he be angry about that? That don't make sense."

Gil licked his suddenly dry lips. Then he confessed, "It does when you know that we shared a motel room."

"Oh."

"Nothing happened! We had no choice. We couldn't go any farther and there was only one room."

"You explained that to Crawford?"

"Yeah, and his son, Pete, backed me up."

"Good."

"No, that's not good." When Rafe stared at him, he tried to explain the culmination of the argument. "What I mean is, he believed me. Not his daughter. Well, Lindsay didn't exactly explain. She wanted him to trust her. Instead, he trusted me."

"Aw. How did she react?"

"About how you'd expect. She has a temper like her father." But she was a hell of a lot prettier. He grinned, knowing she'd condemn that thought.

"That's too bad. She's a nice lady," Rafe said, rubbing his chin, as if thinking about what he'd heard.

"Yeah. And then I treated her rotten today."

"It'll be a wonder if she ever comes home again."

Gil felt his heart sink. Not that it mattered to him, personally, he hurriedly assured himself, but Lindsay deserved better than that.

When he parked at the Crawfords, he didn't see Lindsay's car. But she'd probably put it in one of the barns, out of the way. He hoped he'd have an opportunity to speak to her privately right away. He'd feel better when he'd had a chance to apologize.

Otherwise he might get indigestion.

Mrs. Crawford greeted them at the door, welcoming them warmly. The minute they stepped into the house, Caleb and his sons, three of them at least, did the same. Gil couldn't help but contrast that with Lindsay's welcome the night before.

All the way to Oklahoma, he'd dismissed Lindsay's comments about her family. Maybe he still thought she'd overreacted a little, but he could see her point.

Mrs. Crawford invited them to sit down. She'd prepared some hors d'oeuvres.

Gil and Rafe did so, and Caleb immediately launched into a discussion on winter feed, joined enthusiastically by his sons. Gil remembered Lindsay's comment when he'd talked about his place, that he reminded her of her father and brothers.

Though he kept watching the door for Lindsay's arrival, he talked with the others. After all, he loved ranching, but he could discuss other topics, too.

Lindsay didn't arrive.

When Mrs. Crawford invited them all to the table, he finally asked the question that was driving him crazy.

"Where's Lindsay?"

The two older Crawfords exchanged a look. Then Mrs. Crawford finally said, "I'm sorry, Gil. But when she got home, Lindsay said she'd already made plans and couldn't cancel. I know I should've called you, but we were looking forward to getting to know you. I hope you don't mind.''

"No, of course not. I'm enjoying the evening," he said with a smile. Inside, he was tied in knots. Did Lindsay really have plans, or was she so mad at him she wouldn't even eat dinner in the midst of her family?

He suddenly realized Pete was talking.

"She and Kelly have been friends forever."

"Kelly?" Gil asked. He'd missed the first part of Pete's words. Was Kelly a man or a woman?

Pete cocked one eyebrow. "Kelly Hampton. The two of them have been best friends since first grade," he said. "I never really understood why. They don't have much in common."

"Me, neither," Caleb agreed. "Her mother seems a nice enough lady, but not our kind."

Carol looked sternly at her husband and son. "She is a nice lady, and it's not her fault that her husband walked out, leaving her with a baby and no way to make a living except waiting tables."

Caleb shrugged.

Pete looked at his mother. "She never brought Kelly around here much. How would we know if she's a nice person?"

"When Lindsay did bring any friends here, you teased them unmercifully, Peter," Carol said, staring down her son. "No wonder she didn't want to invite friends over."

"Aw, Mom, we were just havin' fun."

Gil watched the interplay, storing away the information. Lindsay had had a lot of benefits from her family, but she'd had some disadvantages, too.

"So, is Kelly male or female?" he asked, trying to make his voice sound casual.

Apparently he failed miserably, since all the Crawfords gave him sympathetic smiles. Pete answered, "She's a lady, pal. A widow with a little boy."

Gil didn't know how to respond. He certainly didn't want to give his honest reaction, a sigh of relief. That would give the Crawfords the idea that he cared. Of course, he did, but not—not romantically. He certainly didn't want to raise any expectations in that area.

Fortunately, Carol urged them all to the table which meant he didn't have to respond. Rafe met his gaze and gave him a wink, letting him know he recognized his dilemma. That communication made him feel good, not alone.

Had Lindsay ever experienced that much closeness with her family? He found that a sad thought.

After a pleasant meal, and a little more conversation, Caleb offered to show Gil some horses he had housed in the barn because they were either injured or due to foal any day.

"I'd love to see them, Mr. Crawford, but we've taken up too much of your evening as it is. We should be going."

"Don't be silly, boy," Caleb said with a smile. "We figured you'd want to stay 'til Lindsay got back. She shouldn't be too much longer. Come on."

Not leaving him a choice, without being rude, Caleb walked from the room, expecting him to follow. Gil figured he'd already used his quota of rudeness for the day, so he nodded at Rafe, thanked Mrs.

Crawford for the wonderful dinner again, and headed to the barn.

He didn't mind waiting for Lindsay's return.

Lindsay hugged Kelly goodbye and hurried out to her car. It had gotten colder since she'd reached Kelly's trailer house.

But they'd had a good evening. She realized how much she missed talking to Kelly. They knew each other better than anyone in the world. It had only taken Kelly a few minutes to figure out something had happened to Lindsay.

Then they'd discussed Gil Daniels nonstop.

But they'd also managed to talk about Kelly's store, and the problems she was facing. Lindsay couldn't help being interested in them. She'd once thought she'd like to have her own store.

In fact, she still wanted to do that. While she'd learned a lot at Bloomingdale's that she'd never learned at school, she still wanted to be in charge. Kelly teased her about always wanting to be the boss.

Maybe she got that from her dad.

Kelly's situation made her sad, too. It had been a real effort for Kelly to attend college. But for three years, she and Lindsay had been roommates. Then Kelly had fallen in love with Dave Hampton and they'd married. Even Lindsay hadn't known her friend was pregnant at the time. Before Andrew was born, Dave had died in a car wreck.

Kelly hadn't been able to return to school, not with the baby and the responsibilities she had then. So she'd opened her store, sinking what savings she had into it.

But she needed an investor, or a partner, Lindsay decided, thinking about it as she drove through the night. Someone to put some money into the operation and also give Kelly a break from the burdens she carried.

Like a lightbulb going on over her head, Lindsay suddenly knew *she* was the one Kelly needed. She could be Kelly's partner. They understood each other. And she had some money.

It would make it possible for her to return to Oklahoma, close to her family, but not be dependent on her parents. Excitement built inside her as she considered every aspect. Of course, she'd have to talk to Kelly about it first. But it was a perfect fit!

She was so distracted when she reached home, she almost didn't notice the strange pickup parked by the house. It couldn't be Gil's, since it was already almost ten o'clock. Ranch folks didn't visit late. The sun came up early.

But who else could it be?

She opened the door to the house, responding to her mother's call. It hadn't come from the kitchen but from the den.

She stepped to the door of the big room and had her answer at once. Both Gil and Rafe were seated among her family.

Before she could even speak, her father leapt to his feet. "Rafe, let me show you a book I got last week on the latest breeding techniques." He grabbed the man by the arm and led him toward the door. "'Bout time you got home, little girl," he said to Lindsay in passing.

"Boys, I could use some help in the kitchen,"

Carol announced. Lindsay watched the shocked expressions on her brothers' faces. Usually Carol chased them out of the kitchen, rather than invite them in.

Gil stood as the others followed Carol. In only seconds Lindsay and Gil were the only occupants in the room.

"Lindsay, I came to apologize for my behavior today," he said rapidly, as if he figured she wouldn't give him much time.

She fought the relief that filled her. She didn't want to be mad at Gil. But she knew better than to let down her guard. "Thank you. I appreciate that."

"I hope you didn't mind my coming to dinner this evening," he said, watching her.

She returned his gaze, her chin lifting. "Of course not. Mother is free to ask whomever she pleases to dinner."

With a small grin, he took a step closer to her. "You know she asked me here because of you."

She held her ground. "Yes, but she didn't ask me. I'm afraid I'd already made plans."

"I heard. Did you have a good visit?"

His interest surprised her. And relaxed her just a little. "Yes. Kelly and I are good friends. I've missed her."

"Yeah. I don't know what I'd do without Rafe."

Her smile deepened. Maybe he did understand.

"When are you heading back to Chicago?"

That question halted her melting resistance to Gil's charms. And threw her mind into turmoil. "I'm not sure. I had thought to leave tomorrow, but I may take an extra day or two."

"That would be great," he said with a smile.

Why? Did he want her to stay? No, she knew better. He was just being polite. "We'll see."

"I'd like to have you come back to the ranch, maybe discuss the ideas you had about fixing up the house. It's time I did something to it."

She stared at him. Having figured out that his anger had been connected to his ex-wife, she was surprised at his words. "Why?"

"As I said, it's time. Poor Rafe doesn't handle the cold as well as he used to, and I promised him I'd do something about the drafts."

He smiled, but Lindsay wasn't fooled. "Then you probably need to talk to a contractor, instead of me."

"Sure, I wasn't expecting you to swing a hammer, Lindsay," he said with a chuckle…and another step closer to her. "But I thought you might have some good ideas about how to improve the place. After all, your parents' house is up-to-date, well done."

A little friendly exchange, that's all he wanted. And Lindsay liked to help people out. But she didn't want to spend time with Gil. Not when it would only make her want him more. "Mom would be the better person to ask. She's great at that kind of thing, and she'll be around."

"I'd be grateful for her advice, but…I thought it would be nice if you came back to visit before you left. I—I've got some things I'd like to send to Kathy."

"Have you talked to her since we got here?"

"Nope. We only talk every once in a while. But I'm sure she's okay." He frowned, as if he felt guilty.

"Not even to wish her a happy Thanksgiving?" She didn't say it, but the thought occurred again. He was just like the men in her family.

"Yeah, I guess I should've done that, but we got here so late, and I was tired. I'll call her first thing in the morning." He took two steps forward, which brought him almost within reach of Lindsay.

"Good. I think she'd like that." Kathy talked about her brother a lot.

He nodded in agreement and stepped close enough to catch both her hands in his. "I enjoyed having you visit today. I'm sorry it ended so badly."

"I wasn't trying to interfere," she said softly. "It's your place. I just got excited about the house."

"I'm lucky you'd even sit down and eat. It's not in good shape. I—I had a thing about fixing it up because my ex-wife—she wanted to be in *Architectural Digest,* so our apartment was a showplace. I was never comfortable there."

Lindsay had known his anger was connected to his ex-wife. No wonder he didn't want to associate with any woman. He shouldn't until he'd dealt with his anger. It was a good thing she was going back to Chicago.

"You'll probably want to wait until spring anyway," she said with a shrug. "That will give you plenty of time to make a decision."

"Maybe." He tugged on her hands, throwing her off balance, until she fell against him. Then he wrapped his arms around her. "What I can't wait for is to tell you again how sorry I am for my behavior."

"Really, Gil, it's—"

His lips cut off her dismissal of his second apology.

That connection that only grew stronger each time he touched her encouraged Lindsay to slide her arms around his neck, to open her mouth to his insistent lips, to draw even closer to his strong form. As she did so, he reslanted his mouth over hers and took the kiss to new depths. Even their kiss last night, in the car, hadn't been as deep, as long, as—as passionate as this kiss.

Panicked at the loss of control that was growing by the minute, Lindsay pulled back, sliding her hands to his chest to give her breathing room.

"Gil, I don't think—"

"Good," he agreed with distraction, his gaze fixed on her lips. "That's best." Then he kissed her again.

Lindsay couldn't help herself. Being in Gil's embrace was the most exhilarating thing she'd ever experienced. Being surrounded by his big body, his masculine scent, made reality a distant memory. She'd told herself her feelings for Gil had no future. But she had trouble remembering that when he swept her into his arms.

Gil released her mouth. "Good thing I hadn't kissed you like that when we shared a bed," he murmured, his breath shallow and rapid. "We never would've left the motel."

She couldn't argue that statement. She didn't believe in promiscuity, but whatever it was that she and Gil shared made good sense too hard to remember.

His mouth lowered again and she met him more than halfway, eager to draw closer to him again. The man was addictive. She never wanted to stop kissing him.

He seemed to feel the same way. His big hands were stroking her body, encouraging her to get closer, if that were possible. She wanted to touch him, too. Her hand slid into the open neck of his shirt, loving the warmth of his skin, the silkiness of his chest hair. Her other hand began manipulating the buttons on his shirt to allow her more access.

In fact, she was so buried in the desire that spurred her on, she didn't hear the approaching footsteps that normally would've alerted her to someone's presence.

It was only when her father cleared his throat that she vaguely realized they weren't alone.

"Ahem. I guess you two have made up. Maybe you have an announcement to make?" Caleb Crawford asked with great enthusiasm.

Chapter Nine

Anger rose in Gil.

Okay, so it was his fault. He knew what kind of father Caleb Crawford was. He knew kissing Lindsay like he had, in Caleb's house where they could be discovered, was dangerous. He knew he hadn't been able to stop himself.

So he bit his tongue and said nothing. He hated being manipulated. His ex-wife had been an expert at it. But he did realize that Caleb had a right to be protective over his daughter. And he'd rather have the confrontation now than later, because he doubted he could keep himself from kissing Lindsay.

"No!" Lindsay exclaimed, her gaze flicking from her father to Gil and back to her father. "No, Daddy. We had this discussion last night, remember?"

"Then it seems to me there's an awful lot of kissing going on for no reason." Caleb Crawford didn't look happy. Then he roared, "Carol? You'd better get in here!"

Gil leaned closer to Lindsay. "I'm sorry."

The look she sent his way didn't show appreciation for his sentiments. In fact, she looked as though she wanted to scratch his eyes out.

"What's wrong?" Carol asked. She was followed by Lindsay's three brothers.

"These two were smooching like nobody's business, but now they don't have anything to tell me," Caleb protested, frowning at Lindsay and Gil.

The man was formidable. Gil was amazed that Lindsay had stood up to her father as much as she had. He stepped in front of Lindsay, as if to shield her from the heat in her father's glare. "Mr. Crawford, Lindsay and I share an attraction, but we've only known each other three days." Even as he said it, he couldn't believe he hadn't had more time with Lindsay. He felt he understood her as he'd never understood a woman. And yet she was still a mystery.

"Then maybe you should think about that before you start kissing her," Caleb snapped.

Gil wanted to protest, but he decided silence might serve him better.

Lindsay thought differently. "I'll ask you again, Dad. Do you set down the same rules for your sons? How many women have you kissed, Pete?" she demanded, suddenly swerving her glare from her father to her brother.

"Uh, hey, this isn't about me," Pete protested. Rick and Joe began backing up, as if hoping to sneak away, before they, too, could be questioned.

"It never is," Lindsay returned.

Gil heard the bitterness in her answer and wondered that no one else seemed to notice.

"Now, Lindsay, your father is trying to protect you," Carol said soothingly.

With great dignity, Lindsay turned to face Gil. "Thank you for your apology. I'm afraid I owe you a larger one for my family's behavior. I'll check on Kathy when I get back to Chicago." Then she shoved her way past her family and disappeared.

Gil found himself suddenly in enemy territory after being warmly welcomed earlier in the evening. And it made him mad. Lindsay was right. Were her brothers forbidden to kiss a woman unless they were proposing to her?

Lindsay was being treated like a criminal because she exchanged several kisses with someone she was obviously attracted to. No wonder she'd moved all the way to Chicago to get away from the family she loved. She'd told him earlier that she intended to stay an extra day or two. He would guess that her plans had abruptly changed.

Now she would probably leave first thing in the morning.

"Are you people crazy?" Those words burst out of him before he could consider their effect.

"Watch your mouth, boy!" Caleb roared.

"I'm not one of your children, Caleb Crawford," Gil protested even as Rafe moved over to take his arm and try to lead him from the room. "If I were and you treated me like you do Lindsay, I'd move far away, too. Don't you understand what you're doing to her?"

"I love my daughter!" Caleb protested.

"Of course you do, dearest," Carol said, patting her husband's arm. She turned to Gil. "My husband may be a little overprotective, but it's only because he loves her so much."

"You have to protect the womenfolk," Pete added. "You know how it is. You've got a sister. That's why you went to Chicago, isn't it? To protect her?"

Gil had never thought about his behavior toward Kathy before. Had she resented his trip? His concern?

"Best we leave," Rafe whispered, still urging him to the door before the discussion went any further.

He remembered Lindsay's dignified retreat. "Thank you for your hospitality, Mrs. Crawford. I apologize for any—disturbance I've created." He nodded to the men and he and Rafe left the room. He figured the neighborliness that had been extended would disappear now.

To his surprise, Caleb followed him to the door. "No hard feelings, Daniels. I know how it is with an attractive woman. Lindsay doesn't understand the temptation she represents."

Gil's anger bubbled over. "So now, you're not only condemning her for kissing me, you're making it all her fault? Damn it, man, you're supposed to be loyal to her, not me! *I* initiated the kissing. *I* wrapped my arms around her. *I* persuaded her to kiss me back. Don't you dare blame Lindsay!"

Caleb seemed taken back at Gil's vehemence, but Gil was beyond caring about his relationship with his neighbor. "Hate me if you want. But don't condemn

Lindsay because I kissed her without offering marriage!''

Pete stepped forward. ''So you're saying you were just having fun with my sister? You don't have any serious intentions?''

Gil sighed in exasperation. These people just didn't get it. ''Pete, I'll ask you what Lindsay asked you. Have you ever kissed a woman without offering marriage?''

''Yeah, but she wasn't my sister!'' Pete roared. Then he thought about what he'd said. ''Of course I wouldn't kiss my sister. I didn't mean— You know what I mean, damn it!''

''Your sister is a smart, beautiful woman. I think it's about time someone around here recognize that and let her live her own life.''

He didn't wait for a response, afraid if he stayed he'd end up offering to marry Lindsay to get her away from her well-intentioned family. How anyone could mess up so when they intended to help, he didn't know.

Rafe followed him and slid behind the wheel. ''I'll drive. You might run us off the road.''

Gil didn't argue. He was a little upset about the end to the evening. For a lot of reasons.

After ten minutes of silent driving, Rafe drawled, ''Interesting evening.''

Gil's only response was a grunt.

''I see what you mean about Lindsay's family. They don't give her much support, do they?''

''Nope, and they do it in the name of love!'' After a pause, he asked, ''Do I do the same thing to Kathy?''

"No, boy. You worry about her, but mostly you leave it up to her to let you know if she's in trouble. You assume the best. Those people assume the worst."

Gil wasn't sure he deserved Rafe's support this last trip. He'd pretty much assumed the worst when Kathy called him crying.

With a sigh, he said, "I think tonight's debacle will insure that Lindsay returns to Chicago right away."

"Didn't you expect that?"

"She said something before, uh, before her dad came in about staying another day or two."

"Does it matter to you?"

Gil didn't want to answer that question. He didn't want it to matter. He'd promised himself he'd never let another woman get under his skin, cause him pain. He cleared his throat. "I want Lindsay to be happy."

"If you asked Caleb, I'm sure he'd say the same thing," Rafe said with a wry tone.

Gil couldn't argue with him. But he wanted to.

Before she fell into bed that night, Lindsay packed her bags. Even if she talked to Kelly and stayed in Oklahoma, or moved back eventually, she wouldn't be living with her parents.

As much as she loved them, she couldn't remain under her father's roof, to be treated like a witless child.

Then she crawled into bed and stared at the ceiling in the darkness, thinking about those minutes in Gil's arms. She couldn't regret that interlude, even if it had brought another argument with her father.

But she did regret the heartbreak she was facing. How could she fall in love at all with a man like her father, much less fall for him in only three days? Those first few hours in the car, if someone had told her she'd fall for Gil Daniels, she would've laughed. It must be infatuation, she decided. She couldn't have *really* fallen in love.

She'd probably fallen in lust.

The man was a top-notch kisser. He could make Lindsay forget everything. And want more.

So, she determined, she could talk to Kelly about becoming her partner, but she couldn't live at home. And most important of all, she had to avoid Gil Daniels. She'd leave in the morning, stopping on her way to talk to Kelly. Even if they did decide to become partners, she'd have to return to Chicago anyway. But she'd stay away from Gil and her parents. With those resolutions, the pain in her battered heart eased a little. She could handle those two things.

First thing the next morning, she discovered how impossible her resolutions were. When she'd dressed, she gathered her bags to come down to the kitchen. As she entered the room, her mother looked up.

"You're leaving?"

"Yes, Mom. It's a long drive back."

"But—but your father wanted to show you some things around the ranch."

"I doubt he still wants to, Mom. After all, we didn't part on good terms last night." She didn't say any more because she didn't want to think about how her evening had ended.

Before her mother could reply, the phone rang. Since Lindsay was standing near it, she answered.

"Lindsay? Are you okay?"

She recognized Gil's voice at once. "Haven't we had this conversation before?" she asked, trying to keep her voice light.

"Yes, we have, but what's your answer?" Gil persisted.

"I'm fine."

"When are you leaving?"

Lindsay bit her bottom lip. She didn't want to lie to him, but he hadn't specifically asked when she was leaving Oklahoma. Just when she was leaving. And she was definitely leaving her family this morning.

"I'm already packed." That was definitely not a lie.

"You promised you'd take something to Kathy for me," he reminded her.

Yes, she had. She tried to escape that promise. "I really don't have time—"

"Why don't you come here and have an early lunch? It will keep you from having to stop for a while. In fact, we'll pack you some sandwiches so you won't have to stop for food at all until in the morning. Please?"

Lindsay sighed, and gave in. "Okay, I'll be there at eleven. Whatever it is, it's not big, is it? You know how little space I have."

"I know," he assured her with a chuckle. "I didn't think I'd be able to stand up straight after that ride."

"It wasn't that bad, Gil," she returned, but she laughed, too.

"Right, I'll see you at eleven."

"Yes." After their goodbyes, she hung up the phone and turned to her mother, only to discover she'd disappeared. She'd probably gone to the barn to tell Caleb about his daughter's departure.

Lindsay shrugged. She'd tried. She loved her family, but their attitudes frustrated her so much. It was hard to be happy when you didn't receive any respect from those you loved.

She fixed herself a bowl of cereal and sat down at the breakfast table. Maybe she'd have time for her father to show her around before she left for Gil's. After all, it was only a little after eight o'clock.

A shout penetrated the walls of the kitchen, alarming Lindsay. She leapt to her feet to look out the window that gave a view of the barn. Her brother Rick was racing to the house.

Lindsay ran to meet him. Something was wrong.

"Lindsay, call the doctor. Mom fell and Dad thinks she broke her arm. We're going to take her in."

Though she wanted to go to her mother, she did as Rick asked. Then she ran upstairs and grabbed a blanket and a pillow, meeting her father and mother just as they got to the car her mother usually drove.

"Should I go with you?" she asked as she wrapped the blanket around her mother and helped her inside the car.

To her surprise, her mother said, "Yes, please, if you have the time."

"Of course I have the time, Mom," she said, ignoring her father's gaze. She settled her mother with the pillow. Then she rounded the car to slide in beside her.

"What happened?" she asked as her father got behind the wheel and slammed his foot on the gas pedal.

With a wince her mother spoke to her husband first. "Caleb, please slow down. The bumps," she paused to gasp, "make my arm hurt more."

Though he didn't want to, as Lindsay saw the reluctance on his face, he said, "Yes, dear," and did as she asked.

"Did you fall?" Lindsay asked.

"Yes. It got below freezing last night and there was a little ice I didn't notice. Before I knew it, my feet flew over my head."

"But, honey, why were you coming out to the barn?" Caleb asked, frowning as he looked in the rearview mirror.

Carol, her eyes closed, muttered, "To tell you Lindsay was leaving right away."

Lindsay bit her bottom lip.

Her father turned his head to stare at her.

"Dad, the road," she reminded him as the car headed for the ditch alongside the drive.

He jerked his head and the steering wheel, putting the car back on track. "Were you going to leave without saying goodbye?" he asked angrily.

"No," Lindsay assured him. "I intended to come out to the barn to see you. But Gil called and Mom headed for the barn before I hung up."

"You still mad about last night? I was trying to protect you," her father insisted.

Lindsay sighed. Her father would never understand.

With that realization came a release of tension. If she accepted that fact, maybe she could stop fighting her father. He was never going to see her as an adult. But that didn't mean she had to stop acting like one whenever they were together.

"No, Dad, I'm not mad. But I'm an adult. Visiting is fine, but I can't come home again."

"Of course you can!" her mother said sharply. "We've kept your room for you."

Lindsay didn't know whether to laugh or cry. As if the only problem was whether there was a place for her to sleep.

"You always have a place with us, little girl," her father said, using his favorite nickname for her. Which summed up her dilemma.

Both her parents suddenly realized what she'd said. Her mother asked, "You were thinking of coming home? To stay?"

"Hey, little girl, that'd be—"

"I can't, Dad, Mom. I'm sorry." She stared out the window, afraid to meet her parents' gazes.

An hour later, Lindsay had to retract her words. Two hours into the morning and she'd already had to recant on both resolutions. She'd agreed to see Gil again. Then, when the doctor took her mother into surgery, saying he had to put a pin in her arm, Lindsay had promised her father she'd stay home until her mother was feeling better.

"What am I going to send to Kathy?" Gil asked Rafe. He'd made up that story last night to insure

Lindsay would visit him again before she left for Chicago.

His friend had come in for a second cup of coffee and was leaning against the kitchen cabinet. "Why would you send her anything?" Rafe asked.

"Because I told Lindsay I needed her to come pick something up for Kathy." He rubbed the back of his neck as he paced the room. "She's coming for lunch at eleven. I told her we'd pack her some supper, too."

"There goes my plan to check fences this morning," Rafe said, but he was grinning.

Gil supposed he was pleased because it was a cold morning with the prospect of rain. "I'll help you with the fences after Lindsay leaves."

"Why don't you send Kathy your parents' wedding album. You can say you didn't want to mail anything so irreplaceable in case it got lost."

"You're brilliant, Rafe!" Gil told him, chuckling. "I'd never have thought of that. Lindsay will believe that story for sure."

"Yeah. But will Kathy?"

Gil stared at his friend. "What do you mean?"

"She's never asked for the album. When you go see her in the next week or two, she's bound to ask why you sent it."

Gil frowned. "I'm not going to Chicago for Christmas," he insisted.

Rafe laughed. "You're going. If Lindsay's up there, you'll be going."

"You're beginning to sound like Caleb Crawford," Gil warned.

"Nope, I'm not trying to force you. I'm predicting

the future. There's a difference.'' Then he set down his coffee cup and began to organize the requirements for sandwiches to pack for Lindsay.

Gil looked at his watch. Then he wished he hadn't. It would be another hour before Lindsay arrived for lunch. Instead of going back out to work, he decided to go upstairs and take a shower, maybe check his stocks. He didn't want to leave the house in case she got there early.

But, of course, her coming wasn't any big deal. Just like her leaving wasn't any big deal.

After all, he knew where she lived. He could go visit his sister anytime he wanted. And see Lindsay.

But probably not before Christmas.

Rafe was way off on that prediction.

Lindsay sat with her father for a few minutes before she realized she'd need to call Gil. She hoped he hadn't fixed any food yet.

"Dad, I have to call Gil. He invited me to lunch on my way back to Chicago.''

"On your way back to Chicago? It's not necessary to go through Apache to get to Chicago.''

"I know, but he asked me to take something back to his sister, and I agreed. To thank me, he offered to feed me an early lunch. I have to let him know I won't be there.''

"All right, but don't be gone long. I don't know when the doctor will be in here.''

Her father tried to hide how worried he was, but Lindsay saw through his pretense. She patted him on the shoulder. "He said it would take a couple of hours, but that the operation was routine. Mom will be fine.''

Her father blinked rapidly and looked away. ''I don't know what I'd do if she wasn't. She's never been in the hospital before, except when she had you kids.''

''I know,'' Lindsay whispered and leaned over to kiss his cheek. ''I'll be right back.''

Lindsay may have realized she couldn't live at home any longer, but she knew she didn't want to be as far away as Chicago. Her parents had a wonderful marriage. Maybe part of the reason she'd tolerated her father controlling her life was that she knew he loved her, and she knew he loved her mother.

It was the kind of marriage she wanted.

The kind Gil Daniels didn't.

She swallowed the tears that filled her throat. This wasn't the time to worry about Gil Daniels. To give herself a little space, a little distraction, she called Kelly first.

''Hi, it's Lindsay. Mom fell and broke her arm, so I'm going to stay a few extra days to take care of her. And I want to talk to you about an idea I had.''

''I'm sorry about your Mom. And I'd love to get together again,'' Kelly assured her. ''Just let me know when. That is, if you don't mind Andrew coming with us. I can't afford any more baby-sitting than I have to have to work.''

''I love having Andrew around. I'll call you tomorrow or Monday.''

''Great. Lindsay, I really am sorry about your Mom, but I'm so glad you're going to be here a little longer.'' There was a loneliness in Kelly's voice that wrenched Lindsay's heart. Her staying was the right thing to do for a lot of reasons.

She promised herself she wasn't counting Gil in the positive column. She wasn't masochistic.

But she couldn't wait to hear his voice.

Chapter Ten

Lindsay slid down into the chair beside her mother's bed. She'd sent her father home as soon as the doctor had reported the operation a success and they'd seen Carol in recovery.

He was going to clean up and come back to have dinner with Carol when, hopefully, she'd be awake. Lindsay would go home while her father was here and change so she could spend the night at the hospital with her mother.

Not exactly how she'd expected to spend the day.

"May I come in?"

She straightened in her chair and stared at Gil, standing just inside the door. "What are you doing here?"

"I brought your mother some flowers," he said in a quiet voice, lifting a vase filled with colorful hothouse blooms.

"That's very nice of you," Lindsay said, rising

and taking the flowers from him. "She's still asleep from the anesthesia they gave her," she said as she set the flowers on a low shelf near the bed.

"Yeah, it usually takes a while to come out of it. But everything went okay?"

"Yes, fine."

"Where's your father?"

"I sent him home to have a shower. He's going to come back and have dinner with Mom while I go home and change. I'm spending the night here with her."

"Ah. I brought those sandwiches Rafe made, in case you were stuck here. Or we can throw those away and I'll take you out to eat."

"Oh, I'm so sorry Rafe went to all that trouble." When she'd called Gil, he'd assured her she hadn't caused any extra work.

He took her hand. "Don't worry about it. Will you share dinner with me?"

Before she could remind herself she'd decided to avoid Gil, she'd agreed. A giddiness filled her that was an added warning that she was making a mistake. "But we should eat the sandwiches Rafe fixed."

"Okay, we'll have a picnic...in the truck. It's getting colder out there and there's a light rain. They're expecting an ice storm by morning."

"I can't leave until Dad gets back."

"I'll go pick up some sodas and something to go with the sandwiches and be back in half an hour. If your dad's not back by then, I'll wait." He smiled, a slow, warm, all-embracing smile that made her want to fall into his arms. But then he could've frowned and she'd feel the same way.

"Okay," she agreed, an unusual shyness filling her.

They stood there staring at each other, neither moving. Then Gil pulled her into his arms.

In spite of all those lectures she'd given herself, the magic of his kisses was too hard to resist. Her arms slid around his neck and she leaned in to accommodate him.

She was as lost in his arms now as she'd been the night before. The hospital ceased to exist. Her problems disappeared. All she could think about was Gil.

"K-Kissing again?" a weak voice asked.

They broke apart, both breathing rapidly.

"Mom! You're awake."

"Yes, I am," she muttered, her eyes half open. "Were you wanting to entertain me?"

Lindsay ignored her mother's ridiculous question. "How are you feeling?"

"Awful."

"Gil brought you flowers. Aren't they beautiful?" She hoped they distracted her mother's attention from what she'd seen when she woke up.

"Beautiful. Thanks."

"I'm glad you like them," Gil responded. "And I'm sorry you got hurt. Lindsay said the surgery was a complete success."

"Yes, but I'll be out of commission for at least several weeks and I'll have to wear a cast for another month or two," Carol wailed, her emotions boiling over.

"It's all right, Mom. I'm going to stay until you get on your feet. I promised Dad."

She was glad she'd made that decision when she saw relief fill her mother's eyes as well as a few tears. "Oh, thank you, dear. I was so worried."

"No problem, Mom."

"Where is your father?"

"He went home to clean up. He'll be back to have dinner with you. Then I'll be here to stay with you all night."

"I'm sure that's not necessary—"

"Yes, it is," Lindsay said with a smile. "Remember when I had my appendectomy? You stayed with me."

"But you were a child."

Lindsay grinned at Gil. "I was seventeen."

"Definitely a child," Gil assured her with a wink.

A nurse bustled into the room. "You're awake, Mrs. Crawford. How are you feeling?"

"Terrible."

"Would you two step out for a minute while I check my patient?"

While her words were in a question form, Lindsay and Gil both knew it was an order. They moved out of the room. The long hallway was empty, the hospital quiet.

"She seems to be doing pretty well," Gil said, his gaze on her face.

She loved his bright blue eyes. And couldn't help thinking of how they'd looked when he first woke up in the morning.

"Don't look at me like that," he protested with a low groan.

"Like what?" she whispered.

"Like you want to eat me for breakfast," he muttered and pulled her back into his arms, his lips covering hers.

She wasn't sure how long they stood there, tasting each other, touching, pressing together, but they were again interrupted.

"You two can't stop, can you?" her father growled. "I don't suppose you want to say anything this time, either?"

With her new acceptance of her father's attitude, Lindsay reluctantly left Gil's embrace and smiled at her father. "'Fraid not, Dad. But Mom's awake and asking for you."

He forgot about her behavior at once and charged toward the door.

"Wait, Dad, the nurse—"

He didn't stop.

"He loves her very much," Lindsay said with a sigh.

"Yeah," Gil said, suddenly sounding uncomfortable.

The reaction dampened Lindsay's enthusiasm. Gil wasn't interested in marriage. Lindsay would have to remember that before she lost her heart to him forever. But she wondered if it wasn't already too late.

The next morning, Lindsay had plenty of time to plan her day. And to review the evening just past. They'd had their picnic, her and Gil, in her mother's kitchen. Something in his voice at the hospital had been another reminder that there was no future with their...feelings.

And she couldn't trust herself to remember that when they were alone.

Her brothers had drifted in and out. Pete even sat down and enjoyed one of the sandwiches. He also took the opportunity to complain about the next few weeks.

"What are we going to do without Mom to cook for us?"

"I said I would stay," Lindsay reminded him.

"Thanks a lot. We'll all be dead by the time Mom is better."

In the past, those would've been fighting words. She'd been considered hopeless in the kitchen. Only after she moved to Chicago and began cooking for herself, with no critics looking over her shoulder, had she gained any confidence.

Last night she'd smiled and said, "Then perhaps you'd better take up cooking."

Pete had rejected that idea. "I guess we'll muddle through. We can all eat cereal."

"Three meals a day?" she'd teased, feeling more confident now that she'd found a way to deflect all the teasing and disbelief.

She nodded her head. Just thinking about her conversation with Pete made her feel good. Gil, however, was another matter. She was disturbed by her attraction to the man. Even sitting in her mother's kitchen, she had to fight the urge to touch him.

Was she going out of her mind?

By the time her father arrived to take them home, she'd called Kelly and arranged to come over around one, promising to bring lunch with her. If she was going to cook for her family, she might as well include Kelly and Andrew.

Once her mother was settled on one of the large sofas in the den, a coverlet tucked in over her and pillows behind her, Lindsay headed for the kitchen.

When her brothers got in from the community church they all usually attended, they headed for the kitchen, the aroma drawing them like flies to honey.

"Mom cooked!" Rick said with enthusiasm.

"She couldn't have!" Pete contradicted. "Her arm, remember? Mrs. Brown must've come over, and took pity on us."

"I don't care who cooked," Joe announced. "I'm starved."

"Me, too," Michael echoed.

Lindsay stood ready for them, her arms crossed, in front of the table filled with home-fried chicken, mashed potatoes, beans, a tossed salad, and hot rolls.

They came to a screeching halt and stared at their little sister.

"Uh, Lindsay," Joe said, his gaze going past her to the food. "Who brought in the food?"

"No one."

"I told you Mom cooked!" Rick crowed, moving forward, intending to pass Lindsay and grab a plate.

She put out a hand to stop him.

"Mom didn't cook. I did."

The brothers exchanged looks. Then Pete said, "I don't believe you."

"I don't blame you," she said serenely, "and I wouldn't eat any of it, if I were you. There's plenty of canned foods in the pantry."

"Huh?" Mike said, staring at her as if she'd grown two heads.

"I'm going to Kelly's for lunch. Feel free to eat if you want. But I expect the kitchen to be clean and all the leftover food put away when I get back. If it's not, you *will* be reduced to eating cereal and frozen dinners three meals a day until Mom recovers. Understood?"

All four of her brothers nodded, clearly confused by her take-charge air. And distracted by the smell of fried chicken.

She added, "Mom and Dad are in the den with the football game on. Feel free to join them, but don't forget my warning."

Then she scooped up a picnic basket she'd already prepared and headed for her car, storing up the sounds of her brothers attacking the food like ravenous bears.

She was getting better at this coming home thing.

About three o'clock, Gil couldn't stand it any longer. He got up from the lumpy sofa and started out of the living room.

"Aren't you gonna watch the second game?" Rafe asked, barely looking away from the television set.

"Uh, no, I think I'll, uh, go visit a neighbor."

That brought Rafe's gaze sharply to him, and he could feel his cheeks flushing.

"A neighbor over near Duncan, maybe?"

Gil straightened his shoulders. "It's the only polite thing to do. Mrs. Crawford broke her arm."

"Right. Give her my regards." Polite words, but Gil was distracted by Rafe's pointed smile.

"You could come with me."

"I could. If you need me."

"Not exactly, but—but it would make it look more—more normal. We could even stop in Lawton and pick up a cake or something."

"Yeah, that'd be downright neighborly," Rafe agreed, rising to his feet.

When they'd almost reached the Double C Ranch, Gil cleared his throat. "Uh, remember, we're just being neighborly."

"Right. You mean I shouldn't announce that you've got the hots for their daughter and couldn't sit still?"

Gil turned to protest only to discover Rafe grinning like an idiot. "Thanks a lot, Rafe! I almost ran us off the road."

"Better than living like a zombie."

Gil turned to stare at his friend as he parked the car. "What are you talking about?"

"I'm talking about the way you've been living the past two years, hiding all emotion, not relaxing or having any fun. You've shown more feelings since you came back from Chicago than you have since your divorce."

Gil frowned. "I'm not sure that's good. It makes it easier to get hurt."

"Better hurt every once in a while than dead."

Gil had no comeback for Rafe's remark.

They got out of the car and approached the house, Gil bearing a large chocolate cake in the plastic container the store provided, and Rafe knocked on the door.

Joe answered the door, his head turned back toward the living room, still watching a play from the game on television. "Hi, come on in. The Cowboys just scored!"

Rafe didn't hesitate. "Did they? All right! 'Bout time they found their offense."

Immediately they were absorbed into the Crawford family with no awkwardness.

But also no Lindsay.

They were offered cold fried chicken if they wanted it, and they handed over their chocolate cake. Several of the brothers took a big piece of cake.

"I don't know how you can eat again, after that huge lunch," Carol protested.

Gil saw his opening. He hadn't wanted to come right out and ask about Lindsay, and no one had volunteered any information. "Who cooked?"

"Lindsay," Rick said, awe in his voice. "Man, has she changed! Used to, she couldn't boil water without ruining it. She made the best fried chicken I've ever had and—"

"Rick! You love my fried chicken," Carol protested.

"Aw, Mom, I meant besides yours," the young man quickly amended.

Gil grinned. Nice save.

"Hey, even her cookies were top-notch," Pete added. "I don't know how she found the time to make them, too. Dad said they didn't get home from the hospital until half past ten."

Trying to keep his voice casual, Gil said, "That's

great. Uh, where is she now?" The sudden fear that she might have changed her mind and gone back to Chicago was filling him.

"Over at Kelly's," Joe said before another move in the football game drew their attention back to the television set.

Gil wanted to ask them again to reassure himself that Kelly was a woman. She was drawing a lot of Lindsay's attention.

Not that it mattered to him, of course. He was just there to offer his concern to Mrs. Crawford. Being neighborly.

He looked up to find Rafe grinning at him again. Damn it, the man could read his mind. It was a good thing none of the Crawfords were that perceptive.

The sound of a car approaching had Gil on his feet. He recognized that vehicle. He'd spent long, torturous hours in it just a few days ago.

Carol looked up from her recumbent position on the sofa. "Is that Lindsay?"

"Yeah, I think so," he replied, stepping to the window. As soon as he saw her car, he headed for the door.

"You leaving?" Pete asked, not looking away from the television.

"No, I thought I'd see if Lindsay needed any help carrying things."

All the men in the room, except Rafe, looked at him in surprise.

"What could she need help carrying?" Rick asked, bewilderment on his face.

Suddenly, Pete rammed his elbow into his

brother's side and grinned. "Good idea. Let us know if you need more muscle."

Gil took the opportunity and got out of the room, even as he heard Michael ask what Pete meant. Okay, so maybe he'd been obvious. That didn't mean anything.

"Gil! What are you doing here?" Lindsay asked as she saw him. "I mean, I didn't know you were coming over."

"The hospital said your mother had checked out and I thought it would be neighborly to— I wanted to see you." Then, because that remark seemed too obvious, he added, "You know, to make sure everything was all right."

"Everything's fine. At least, it will be as soon as I see the kitchen."

Gil didn't understand her words. "What do you mean?"

"I told my brothers they'd better clean up after lunch. If they didn't, they'll be eating cereal and frozen dinners for a long time."

"Kind of like our dinner at the motel?" he asked, a grin on his face. The food had been terrible, but the company had been the best.

"Yeah," she agreed with a warm smile. Which was hard to do in the cold wind.

"Let's get inside. You got anything you need me to carry?"

She handed him a picnic basket.

"You went on a picnic?" he demanded as he took her arm and hurried into the house.

"No, I took food in it to Kelly's. I had to cook for the family, so I just cooked a little extra."

"I heard your cookies were great, as well as the chicken."

Lindsay laughed. "If you only knew how much they used to criticize me, making me feel like an incompetent fool. I need to write Abby a thank-you note."

"Abby, your sister-in-law?"

"Yes. She's the one who told me I had to go away to find myself."

They'd reached the house. Lindsay stepped into the big room to check on her mother, who was watching the game with her family. Her brothers welcomed her—Mike even paid her a compliment on the food.

Lindsay smiled when Pete kicked him in the ankle. She knew her brothers. The proof wouldn't be in their words but in their actions. If the kitchen was clean and most of the food eaten, she'd know.

Gil followed her into the kitchen, still carrying the picnic basket. Relief flowed through her as she looked at the kitchen table, bare and wiped clean. She'd won! She spun around and grabbed Gil around the neck and kissed him.

He seemed to have no objection to her celebration. Although he did drop the picnic basket. But as his arms came around her, holding her tight against him, she had no complaints. There was nothing breakable in the basket.

"Is everything all— You two are at it again!" Caleb protested. "Stop that!"

Lindsay drew back from Gil, a shudder going through her. "Um, sorry, Dad. We thought we were alone."

Amazingly, those words put her father on the defensive. "I heard something drop and thought you needed help."

Gil turned to look at her father. "I dropped the picnic basket."

Lindsay stepped closer to her father. She had too much on her mind right now to even think about her father's attempt to restrain her behavior. "Dad, I'm glad you came in here."

Those words surprised both men.

"I need to talk to you. I—I want to buy a building in Lawton. If I can show you the numbers, would you consider making me a loan?"

"Don't be ridiculous!" her father returned, irritation on his face. "What would you do with a building in Lawton? That's out of the question."

Lindsay felt her bubble of exhilaration burst. She'd been so excited after her conversation with Kelly, buoyed by her success with her brothers, that she'd jumped in with both feet. She should've known her father would shoot her down.

"I'll loan you the money," Gil said, moving closer to her.

"The hell you will!" Caleb roared.

Chapter Eleven

Lindsay stared at Gil. "But you haven't even asked any questions," she pointed out. Neither had her father, but he'd also turned down any hope of a loan.

Gil smiled. "You're a smart lady. I know you'll explain everything to me."

Gil's offer proved he trusted her. And trust was more potent than his kisses. Lindsay leaned toward him, awe filling her.

"Here now, none of that. And you're certainly not borrowing money from him!"

Her father's words made her realize what she'd intended to do. She'd already kissed the man once today without warning. She'd better watch herself. It could become habit-forming. "I will if I want to," she said calmly, still staring at Gil. "But I'll probably try a bank first. It would be more professional of me. But, Gil, your offer means a lot. Thanks."

Her father huffed.

"What's going on?" Joe asked, bringing in his empty cake plate.

"Your sister thinks she's going to buy a building in Lawton. Wanted to borrow money from me. And *he* offered to loan it to her!" He pointed an accusing finger at Gil. By the time he finished his roar, Lindsay's other three brothers had joined them, wanting to know what all the yelling was about.

While her father gave them his version of the conversation, Lindsay picked up the picnic basket and began unloading the dirty dishes into the sink. Then she stored the picnic basket in the pantry.

"You can't be serious, Lindsay," Mike said. "There's not going to be a big increase in the real estate market in Lawton. I mean, it's doing well, but you should put your investments in the stock market."

Lindsay smiled at her brother and rinsed the dishes before putting them in the dishwasher.

"There, that's settled," Mike said, smiling at his father.

Lindsay turned around, still smiling. "No, it's not, but it's not really anyone's business but mine, and possibly Gil's if I borrow money from him."

"Lindsay, I forbid you to even consider such a thing!" Caleb shouted.

"Dad, I'm twenty-five, not fifteen."

"But you haven't even explained what you're talking about," he protested.

She cocked her head to one side. "As I recall, you didn't ask before you summarily rejected the idea of helping me."

"Well, I— It just sounds crazy."

"Then it's a good thing you didn't agree, isn't it?"

Gil stepped closer to her. "Does this mean you're thinking about staying in town? Leaving Chicago?"

Lindsay watched his face carefully as she nodded. The sparks that lit up his eyes encouraged her, making her wish they were alone, instead of in a kitchen with all the male members of her family except Logan.

"Caleb?" Carol called from the other room. "What's going on?"

"Come in here and tell your mother what you're talking about doing. We can't leave her out," Caleb insisted.

Everyone trooped after Caleb, Gil included, but he reached out to take Lindsay's hand in his. She smiled warmly, pleased by his support.

Again Caleb filled in the details.

Carol looked at her daughter. "You're thinking of staying? Here?"

Lindsay quickly said, "Not here, exactly. It will take some time, and I'll have to find out about costs, but I think I'll be living in Lawton. Close enough to see you more often," she added hurriedly.

Those words sent her father into another spasm of protests and her brothers delivered a barrage of questions.

Lindsay held up her hand. "Look, I'll tell everyone what I'm hoping to do if you'll be patient." She took a deep breath, knowing in advance that the male members of the family would object.

"I have some money I inherited from Great-aunt Agatha that Dad invested for me. I'm going to go into partnership with Kelly in her dress store. But I think we'd be better off buying the building...for several reasons. We need to expand, and we can build a living space over the store.''

She'd expected the negative response from her father and brothers. But Gil's horrified expression stopped her cold.

''Gil? What's wrong?''

''I didn't know you wanted the money to have a career in fashion, Lindsay.'' He stood stiff and cold, staring at her.

She shook her head at her own silliness. She knew how he felt about fashion, because of his wife. And yet she'd believed him when he said he supported her.

With a painful smile, she said, ''Then I guess the loan idea is off. Thanks anyway.'' With a deep breath, she added, ''Well, I guess I've interrupted football long enough. Thanks, guys, for cleaning up the kitchen. I'll see you later.''

Without looking at Gil, she headed for the stairs and the sanctuary of her old bedroom.

It was another silent drive, this one taking them home. Rafe let Gil drive this time, a good sign, Gil supposed, since it meant he thought Gil wouldn't run them off the road because he was upset.

Gil wasn't so sure. To hear that Lindsay was planning to stay in the area, which thrilled him, only to learn that she intended to involve herself in the fashion industry, sent him on a downward spiral. He had, of course, vowed never to get near a woman who considered her appearance more important than her life.

But he couldn't help remembering the disappointment on Lindsay's face. It reminded him of the times early in his marriage when he had turned to his wife, excitement filling him, and shared an idea with her. But Amanda had rejected everything unless it was her own idea. He had done the same thing to Lindsay. He had erased that excitement from her face and voice.

"You gonna sell any cows in the spring?" Rafe asked.

Gil stared at him. Where had that subject come from? "Of course we'll sell the young bulls at the end of the summer. Not before then."

"Uh-huh. Guess you and Lindsay will be in the same business then."

Gil almost stood on the brakes. "What are you talking about?" Rafe wasn't making any sense.

"You'll both be selling a product. Sounds the same to me."

Gil picked up speed. "It's not the same. Fashion is all about ego. It's an unnecessary thing that only creates problems."

"Vegetarians might say the same thing about raising beef. Or at least some of those things. They sure wouldn't be in favor of it."

"I suppose not, but they're in the minority. All they have to do is not buy beef, instead of trying to convert the world to their way of thinking." He'd wanted to concentrate on his anger, to think about Lindsay's betrayal...about the way he'd betrayed *her*...not discuss fanatics with Rafe.

"Fashion sure cheers up a lot of ladies. And the

men who are watching 'em, too,'' Rafe said, staring straight ahead, not looking at his companion.

Gil immediately pictured Lindsay in her teal suit with that short skirt that showed off her killer legs. ''But it's not necessary.''

''Lots of things aren't necessary. But I'd sure miss a good steak...or a beautiful woman.''

''Rafe, you can't justify what Lindsay's doing! It's unacceptable!'' Gil was sure he was right. She knew how he felt. If she had any interest— What was he thinking about? Of course there was nothing between them. Friendship, that's all it was. And he didn't have to be friends with her.

They reached Gil's ranch and he got out of the truck with relief. When they went in the house, though, Rafe stopped him one more time.

''This isn't about fashion, Gil,'' Rafe muttered.

He spun around and stared at Rafe. ''Of course it is!''

''Nope. This is about whether you trust Lindsay not to leave you. Pure and simple, that's all it comes down to.''

Gil stared at him, the truth slapping him in the face. But he couldn't say anything.

''Women leave men all the time. And men leave women. The reasons change. Bottom line is trust. Does she love me enough to be there for me? Do I love her enough to be there for her? Even if it means a sacrifice. If the answer is yes, then you should get married. If it's not, then you move on down the road.''

Rafe walked past Gil and disappeared, not waiting for a response.

A good thing. Gil's heart ached. Rafe was right, but Gil didn't want to admit it. Because he didn't have the answer. He didn't know for sure how he felt about Lindsay.

He knew he wanted her.

But for forever? When she was involved in the one industry that had ruined his first marriage?

Though, according to Rafe, that wasn't accurate.

And how did she feel about him? When he'd offered to loan her the money, the look she'd bestowed on him had sent champagne bubbles through him. Her look before she'd left the room had almost destroyed him.

What was he going to do now?

Lindsay spent a lot of time on the phone Monday morning. She'd talked with the only bank in town. The president had agreed to listen to her pitch, but he hadn't made any promises.

He would definitely consider the loan if her father would co-sign. That much he could promise her now.

Lindsay wasn't about to beg her father to do that. Not when he didn't have any faith in her. She thought of Gil's lovely offer, later withdrawn. In that moment, when he'd offered his trust to her, she'd felt she could leap tall mountains in a single bound.

Now she was an ordinary person with big dreams.

"Lindsay?" her mother called from the sofa. Her father had carried her down this morning after Lindsay had helped her clean up and change into a fresh nightgown. The doctor had suggested Carol stay in bed for several days.

"Coming, Mom," she said, hurrying to her side.

When she reached the living room, she expected her mother to ask for a drink, or something to eat, or more blankets. Instead she asked Lindsay to sit down.

"Are you lonely, Mom? I'm sorry, I was just—"

"I heard you."

"What?"

"Calling the bank. Charlie Jones wouldn't agree to the loan?"

"He gave me an appointment for tomorrow morning to hear what I have to say. That's fair enough," she said with a smile that she knew didn't reach her eyes. "I'm working on my numbers now."

"We've banked there for forty years. What's wrong with that man?" Carol protested.

Lindsay shrugged her shoulder. "I don't have your resources, Mom. It's me asking for a loan, not you or Dad."

Carol stared at her. "So he'll give it to you if your father co-signs?"

Lindsay didn't want to answer that question. "We'll see after I talk to him tomorrow."

"I liked your ideas, what you've shared with me," Carol said. She'd asked Lindsay some questions this morning while Lindsay helped her. "I know you want to do this on your own, but if Charlie is stubborn, I'll give him a piece of my mind, and then *I'll* co-sign the papers."

Some of the amazement from Gil's offer was repeated in Lindsay at that moment. But she wasn't going to put her mother in an argument with her father. "Mom, I don't want Dad upset with you."

"Dear, I have my own money, completely in my

control. Charlie has been managing it for all these years after your grandparents died. Either I will co-sign, or Charlie will say goodbye to that account.''

Lindsay stared at her mother. She'd had no idea her mother had any money of her own. ''But, Mom—are you sure it won't upset Dad?''

''It might. But I have the right to decide what to do with my money. I believe you'll do well. And I want you back here in Oklahoma, not in Chicago.''

Lindsay leaned over and hugged her mother. ''Thank you. Now I feel confident about giving in my notice on my condo and my job and arranging packers.''

''Good. The sooner you're here to stay, the better.''

''You do understand that I won't live here at home as soon as we get the apartment ready?''

Carol nodded. ''It will be good for Kelly to get her baby out of that house trailer. They're not safe in tornado country.''

''I know. It's going to be good for her to spend more time with Andrew, too. With both of us at the store and him just up the stairs, we're going to man-age much better.''

''This is what *you* want to do, isn't it, dear? You're not doing this just for Kelly?''

''No, Mom, I'm not doing it for Kelly. She's just a perk.''

''And Gil?''

''I can't be someone I'm not. If Gil has no interest in me, as I am, then the decision is made.''

Her mother nodded and squeezed her hand in sympathy. "I think I'll take a nap now. You go make your arrangements."

Kelly stood, but then she leaned down and kissed her mother's brow. "Thanks, Mom, for trusting me."

"I always have, dear, but your father and the boys made it hard for you to realize it. I love you."

As soon as Lindsay left the room, Carol pulled the phone extension closer to her and dialed the bank's number. "Mr. Jones, please," she said, naming the president.

It only took her about two minutes to make her position clear to her old friend. Charlie hurriedly assured her he'd take care of Lindsay tomorrow.

"Thank you, Charlie," Carol said sweetly. "I knew you'd be helpful."

She hung up the phone and lay back with a sigh of contentment. Her baby was coming home.

Caleb and his sons talked a lot that morning as they made sure the animals had feed and they chopped a hole in the ice over the drinking water.

"I think Lindsay might just make it work," Pete said. "She's been different since she's come home. More grown up. And she can really cook."

"She's not opening a café!" Caleb said with scorn. "She's opening a damned dress store!"

Joe shook his head. "I'm not in favor of it, but you've helped all of us try different things, Dad. Why won't you help Lindsay?"

That question seemed to stop the older man. Then he said, "But I'll take care of her. She doesn't need to take on the worry of her own business."

Even Rick knew better than to agree with his father. "It's a new millennium, Dad. Most women don't just sit around. Besides, Lindsay is kin to both you and Mom."

"Your mother doesn't have a job!" Caleb barked. It had always been a source of pride to him that he'd been able to support his wife.

"No, but she runs the entire town," Pete said with a grin. "She could run for mayor and win hands down."

An hour later, Caleb came back to the house and checked on Carol. She was napping on the couch. He didn't see Lindsay anywhere around. He stepped into the kitchen and picked up the phone and called the bank. When someone answered, he asked to speak to Charlie Jones.

There were chores to be done. They'd been Gil's savior when he'd first bought the ranch. He'd fallen into bed so tired he couldn't think for long about his misery, his failure at his marriage.

Today, he was so tired he couldn't think while he did his chores. He'd lain in bed too long last night thinking about his misery, his failure with Lindsay.

He and Rafe took a break and came into the kitchen for a cup of coffee to warm up. The wind was bitter out there. It wasn't a lot warmer in the house, with all its drafts.

"Sure would be good to fix up the house. Think Lindsay will give you any tips?" Rafe asked as he poured the coffee.

Gil stared straight ahead. "I'll call a contractor I know and see how soon he can get to us."

Rafe stared at him, surprise on his face.

"You're really going to do it?"

"I'm going to get the house shipshape. I'm *not* going to let a decorator get hold of it."

"Suits me. A big hot-water heater, okay? And a good central heating system? If you have enough money?"

"Rafe, I told you the investments are going well. When I finish, you can furnish your part of the house any way you want. You've got plenty of money, too." He gave a small grin at Rafe's look of astonishment. "Haven't you been listening when I told you about your stocks?"

Rafe shook his head. "It's just a jumble of numbers to me. Besides, I trust you."

Those words reminded Gil too much of the fiasco he'd made of his life yesterday. Telling Lindsay he supported her. Then ripping that support right out of her hands when she'd needed it most.

He took a sip of coffee, then set it down. "You think Lindsay will be able to get a loan?"

"Don't know," Rafe said. "Bankers don't have much heart. At least that's what I've heard."

They drank their coffee in silence for several minutes. Then Gil stood up and crossed over to the phone on the wall. He called information. "First National Bank in Duncan."

After the operator gave him the number, he dialed it. When the woman's voice announced the name of the bank, he asked who was president. After she gave him the name, he asked to speak to the man.

"What are you doing, Gil?" Rafe asked.

"I'm making sure Lindsay gets her loan."

* * *

It was still cold the next morning, but Lindsay dressed in her teal suit with the gold buttons. It was the only professional outfit she'd brought with her.

She wished she had her leather briefcase to carry, too, but it was in her apartment in Chicago. She'd spent most of the day yesterday figuring her budget, her ability to repay the loan, and the prospects for their shop.

Her mother assured her she'd be fine on the sofa by herself, but Lindsay had called to make sure the housekeeper would be in that day. "Mrs. Brown should be here any minute, Mom. I'm going to put some cookies and a glass of milk on the table by you, so you'll have a snack."

"I swear, I'm going to put on weight with your cooking. Everything tastes great."

After providing the snack, Lindsay leaned over and kissed her mother's cheek. "Wish me luck."

"Of course, dear, but I have a feeling you won't need it."

Lindsay chalked her mother's confidence up to not knowing much about the business world. Banks were notorious about being stingy with their money. Particularly when it came to loaning money to single women.

Her father came in as she was leaving.

"You going somewhere?"

They hadn't discussed anything since Sunday, so Lindsay simply said, "Yes, I have an appointment."

Her father nodded. "You look...very nice," he said and bent down to kiss her cheek.

"Thanks, Dad," she muttered, fighting to keep

tears from her eyes. Crying wouldn't make her appear professional.

All the way to the bank, she made her arguments over and over in her head. She wanted to have every answer at hand, no matter what the man asked her.

With her head down, she marched toward the front door of the bank and ran into a solid wall of muscle. With a pardon already on her lips, she looked up into Gil's blue eyes.

Chapter Twelve

Having run into Gil outside the bank, Lindsay had difficulty pulling her concentration together. He'd said he was there to do some business, but she didn't understand why he'd be in Duncan and not Apache. Or even Lawton.

The receptionist escorted her to Charlie Jones's office at once. She would've preferred a few minutes to gather herself together.

Charlie greeted her warmly and offered her a chair. With a deep breath, she sat down and spread out the papers she'd prepared. Charlie came around the desk and took the chair next to her so he could see what she'd brought.

She launched into her spiel, glad she'd practiced it several times. Though she watched Charlie's face and thought he approved of what she showed him, she held her breath when she'd finished, waiting for his response.

"Damn, I don't know why I got so many phone calls, Lindsay. I thought maybe you didn't know what you were doing," he said with a big smile.

She stared at him. "I don't understand what you mean."

"Well, first your mother called and threatened to skin me if I wasn't kind to her baby girl."

Lindsay turned a bright red with embarrassment.

"Then your father did the same thing."

"Dad? Dad asked you to give me the loan?"

"I don't remember asking being a part of it," Charlie said ruefully. "And then your young man came in and made a big deposit just so he could tell me how to run my business, too."

Lindsay froze, staring at the man. *Her young man* could only mean Gil. She'd just seen him outside the bank. And he was the only man in the area she'd even looked at, much less kissed in Oklahoma in a long time.

But Charlie wasn't waiting for her to get up to speed. "The crazy thing about all this is your presentation would have earned a loan without all those threats."

Relief flooded Lindsay. "Really? You would've given me the loan without the phone calls?"

"Why not? You've got everything worked out. You're well-trained and talented. Kelly has already shown that she can make it through tough times."

"But we're both single women. I thought—"

"Heck, Lindsay, we're not behind the times. What matters is what you've got to offer. And you have a lot to offer."

Lindsay stuck out her hand to shake his. "Thank

you so much. I wanted to be able to do this on my own. I appreciate the opportunity you're giving me.''

"I'm pleased we can do so. I had my secretary prepare the papers this morning. If you want to go through them and sign them while you're here, we can release the money in about a week.''

"That would be perfect,'' she assured him, a big smile on her lips. Inside, her emotions were all jumbled up, anger mixing with excitement, sadness with exhilaration. But she'd deal with all that later. Now she had business to conduct.

Lindsay went straight from the bank to the shop in Lawton. Kelly was waiting on a customer. She ran the shop alone except for a teenager on Thursday evenings and all day Saturday, to keep expenses down.

When two more ladies entered the shop, Lindsay stored her purse behind the counter and offered her assistance. When the three satisfied customers left the store, Lindsay and Kelly high-fived each other.

"Wow, that's a good morning's worth of sales,'' Kelly crowed, grinning.

"Even better, I got the loan. We'll get a check next week. I'm going to the real estate office to make an offer on the building.''

"No!'' Kelly exclaimed, disbelief on her face.

"Yes! Then I'll call the contractor and get a bid on the work upstairs. If we're lucky, we might be able to move in about the time Mother gets her cast off.''

Kelly hugged her tightly. "I can't believe it. I feel like Cinderella. Oh, Lindsay, that would be so wonderful.'' When she pulled back, she had tears in her eyes. ''We're going to make a great team.''

''Yes, we are. Now, I've got to get home to take care of Mom, after I visit the real estate office. Then I'll call the contractor from home. We've got a lot to do.''

Gil couldn't wait until he heard from Lindsay. *If* he heard from Lindsay. He called the bank president that afternoon.

''Oh, yes, Mr. Daniels. What can I do for you?'' Charlie Jones asked with enthusiasm.

He should show some enthusiasm. Gil had opened a large account that morning. ''I wanted to see if you visited with Lindsay Crawford today.''

''I certainly did. And you had nothing to worry about. She's a smart businesswoman. Had all her ducks in a row. I would've given her the loan regardless.'' Then he hurriedly added, ''Not that we don't appreciate your business, Mr. Daniels. We certainly do. And if there's ever anything I can do to help you in any way, just let me know.''

Gil grimaced. ''Thanks. Glad to hear you're a forward-thinking bank. I appreciate your filling me in,'' he said before he hung up.

Lindsay had gotten her loan. She hadn't even needed his help. Which was good, since she didn't know about it anyway. And he'd keep it that way. But he wished he'd been there to celebrate with her.

When he'd seen her this morning, looking terrific in that suit, he'd wanted to offer her whatever money she needed. He'd wanted to tell her the trust he offered was still there. But there was that small voice that suggested she find another line of work. Sell housewares. Go into real estate. Make pottery.

Anything but fashion.

The phone rang. "Yeah?" he answered, his mind still on Lindsay.

"Oh, Gil!" It was Kathy, crying again.

"Honey, are you all right?" he asked, trying to remember not to expect the worst. To show support, not control. To not be like Lindsay's father.

"Oh, Gil, I'm wonderful! Everything is wonderful!"

She didn't sound wonderful, but he'd take her word for it. Sort of. "Then why are you crying?"

"Gil, we're going to have a baby! That's why I was crying before Thanksgiving."

"You were crying because—"

"No, I was crying because my hormones are out of whack. Brad made me go see a doctor because I've—well, you know, cried, and it upsets him. Isn't it wonderful?"

"Yes, it is, baby sister. It's absolutely astounding."

"Are you happy for us?"

"Of course I am. When are you due?"

"Around the first of August. There's only one thing I'm sad about."

"What's that?"

"Lindsay's not coming back. I'll miss her terribly."

Gil didn't know what to say. He didn't want to tell his sister that he was thrilled Lindsay was staying in Oklahoma. Kathy might think Lindsay meant something to him. She might get her hopes up that her baby would have a cousin some day. That thought stopped him.

"Um, I know you'll miss her." What else could he say? That he was lost in daydreams about a little girl who looked just like her mother?

"I'm going to call her now and tell her. She'll be happy for me."

"I'm sure she will. Look, how about I pay for you and Brad to fly here for Christmas? It's time I got to know your husband better. After all, he's going to be the father of my niece or nephew."

"Oh, Gil, that would be great, but we can afford to—"

"Nope. Part of my Christmas present. Besides, I'm hoping to have some work done on the house before Christmas. You can give me some advice when you get here."

"You know who's really good at that? Lindsay is great at pulling a room together. You should ask her for help."

"Yeah, good idea. Now, go put your feet up. Got to take good care of that baby."

"I will. I love you, Gil."

"I love you, too, baby. Tell Brad hi for me."

He immediately dialed the number of the contractor he knew. He had no time to waste. He couldn't let his pregnant sister catch a cold in his drafty old house.

"Powell Construction," a deep voice announced.

"Hey, Jase, don't tell me business is so slow you're answering the phones these days," Gil teased. He and Jason Powell had become good friends when Jason had built his barn for him.

Jason chuckled. "Not hardly. Secretary's on her coffee break. In fact, business is great right now. How are you, Gil?"

"Good. But I've got a project for you. My house."

With a whistle, Jason said, "That's not a small project."

"Nope."

"Can it wait?"

"My sister's coming for Christmas. I'd at least like a good heating system and enough work to limit the drafts by then. You got something else cooking?"

"Yeah, but I can handle both jobs. Lindsay Crawford just hired me to remodel a building in Lawton. You probably don't know her but—"

"I know her."

"Ah." There was a pause. Then Jason said, "Good-looking woman."

Gil ground his teeth. "Yeah."

He knew his friend recognized the tension in his voice. But he didn't intend to explain anything.

"Can I come out to your place after lunch tomorrow?"

"Come for lunch. Rafe and I aren't gourmet cooks, but we'll fix something."

"Great, see you then."

Lindsay had a million things to do. All she could think about was Gil. She'd decided to write him a note, thanking him for his attempt to help her.

She'd already thanked both her parents. The anger that had filled her at their lack of faith had been resolved. She could even admit that if her child had been facing a challenge, she would be tempted to ease the way. But she knew that wasn't the best thing to do.

She could appreciate their support, though. She and her father actually had a long talk. He explained that it wasn't his lack of faith in her abilities, but the fact that he wanted to take care of her, as he did her mother.

Lindsay had hidden a grin at that remark. She was beginning to have a much better appreciation of her mother's skills. Not only was she one of the most influential people in town, on every board of every business and charity, but she also managed to convince her husband that she was a lady of leisure, totally dependent on him.

After only being home a week, Lindsay was pleased that she understood her parents better, dealt with her brothers' teasing, and felt appreciated for what she'd accomplished.

And all she could think about was Gil.

Once, all those accomplishments would've been enough. Once, finding a new career and forming a partnership with her best friend would've thrilled her.

Once, she hadn't known Gil.

With a sigh, she reread the stiffly worded note, then signed her name, sealed it and put a stamp on the envelope. The fact that he made the effort even when he was against her going into fashion was impressive. She wanted him to know she appreciated it.

She also wanted him to know their thing, whatever it had been, was over. She wasn't going to give up her business for his outdated ideas, his hang-ups.

But she'd miss him.

* * *

Lindsay flew back to Chicago to talk to Bloomingdale's and pack more suitcases. Her limited wardrobe had gotten old quickly.

She spent one evening with Kathy and Brad, celebrating their coming parenthood with them. Kathy promised to water her plants until she could come pick them up and arrange for a mover. She had until the end of December.

Then she returned home. Her mother was up and around now, but not able to fix meals. So Lindsay spent her days at the store, organizing, selling, planning with Kelly and supervising the work done on the building. In the evenings she cooked, but her brothers did the cleanup, much to Carol's surprise.

Joe asked her to bake something for the church's bake sale, but he agreed to come into the kitchen and help. Mike asked her to go shopping with him. He needed to look more professional. Rick asked advice about a young woman he'd started dating. Even Pete showed appreciation for his little sister's abilities.

Her father still called her little girl, but he didn't try to make decisions for her. Well, not often. She even asked his advice on the remodeling. Her mother visited the store frequently, doing all her shopping there.

"I swear, our sales totals have doubled since your mom started shopping here," Kelly said one day. "I feel like we're taking advantage of her."

"But she looks good," Lindsay assured her friend with a grin. "She's great advertising, anyway. She goes everywhere, and she always tells everyone where she buys her clothes."

"I know. Do you think we should—"

Kelly stopped and stared over Lindsay's shoulder. Curious, she turned around. In the midst of all their elegant garments, feminine attire, stood a big cowboy, his hat in his hand.

"Gil! What—can I help you?" Lindsay asked, trying to keep her voice professional. What she really wanted to do was run into his arms. But she couldn't do that. He wouldn't want her to do that.

"I got your note."

He didn't look particularly pleased about receiving it, she noted. "Good. I appreciated the effort—especially in the circumstances."

There was an awkward silence. Lindsay could tell he'd interpreted her words as she'd meant them. Their—whatever it had been, madness, infatuation, longing—was over.

Finally he said, "Um, I thought I'd buy something for Kathy."

"Of course." He wasn't here to see her. He was shopping. "Do you have any idea what you'd like?"

"Nope. I was hoping you could pick something out for me."

Lindsay tried to focus on Gil's sister, but all she could see was Gil. She turned to look around the store for inspiration and knew immediately what she would sell him.

"Is this for a special occasion?" It had suddenly occurred to her that Gil might not know about the baby.

"It's to celebrate the baby."

Now that that was cleared up, she led him across the store to a new shipment they'd just gotten in.

"This would be perfect," she said, lifting one of the jumpers from the rack. "It's the latest style, but it has a relaxed fit. She'll be able to wear it for quite a while, but it's not maternity clothes."

Gil looked at the jumper and then her. "But it's denim. I figured you'd sell me something silk."

"I can, if you want, but I think Kathy would like this. Denim is very popular."

"And washable," Kelly added, standing nearby. "As a mother, I can tell you that becomes very important."

"Okay, I'll take it. And you might pick out a few more things for her for Christmas. She and Brad are coming here for the holidays."

"That's wonderful!" Lindsay exclaimed. "I'd love to—I mean, please tell her to call me when she gets to town," she finished, tempering her enthusiasm. After all, Gil hadn't contacted her since a week· ago. He didn't want her in his life.

"Yeah. I've started renovations on my house."

"Jason said you did," she said with a smile. "That's a wonderful idea."

He shuffled his boots, an amazing reaction from the confident, sexy Gil. Then he looked at her. "Kathy said you'd be the best one to give me ideas about fixing up the house."

Oh, how she wanted to. She'd love to be a part of Gil's life, to share ideas, interests, to— But she couldn't. "There are lots of people who can help you. Jason works with a decorator who's very good."

"No! Never mind. You've got a nice place here,"

he said, more to Kelly than her. Then he took his package and left.

"You were kind of tough on him," Kelly said. "He seems so unhappy."

Lindsay said nothing.

Two days later, Gil returned to the shop. He'd overnighted Kathy's present to her and she'd loved it. He felt it would only be polite to thank Lindsay. Rafe agreed with him. Of course, he'd given him that knowing smile, but Gil ignored it.

"Gil!" Lindsay said as she turned away from helping a customer. "I didn't see you come in."

"You busy?"

There was no one else in the store, so he figured she couldn't claim the need to tend to customers. And Kelly was there.

"Um, I have a lot to do, but I can wait on you."

"I wanted to take you out for a cup of coffee."

She opened her mouth and he read refusal in her eyes. But Kelly intervened.

"Good," Lindsay's partner said, stepping over. "And I'll let you stay gone longer if you'll promise to bring me back a cup."

"That's a deal," Gil said, taking Lindsay's arm. It was the first time he'd touched her in two weeks. His heart beat faster.

Lindsay stared first at him and then at Kelly. Finally, she said, "I have to get my coat."

Once they were seated at the local coffee bar, she made small talk, asking about Rafe and the work on his house. Gil patiently waited her out. When she'd finally run out of anything to say, he muttered, "I'm going crazy."

Her head snapped up and she stared at him. "What did you say?"

"You heard me. Rafe says I'm useless. I can't seem to concentrate on work." It was interesting that her cheeks flamed with color at his confession. "I keep thinking about you."

Instead of expressing similar feelings, which had been his hope, she said, "I have to get back to work."

His hand shot out to catch hers. "Wait! I know I—I didn't stand by you. I have—had a hang-up about—you know. But I don't want to give up our— our friendship." He couldn't call it what he thought it really was. A courtship. He wanted her in his life. But she'd really freak out, then.

"Gil, we don't have a friendship," she told him, her features stiff with rejection.

"Could we? Have a friendship, I mean?"

Then he waited, holding his breath 'til she answered.

Lindsay's heart sank. Friendship with Gil. She wished life could be that simple. But it couldn't be. They'd gone beyond the friendship stage when he kissed her. Things had broken down before they'd gotten to the next stage. The one where she could throw herself in his arms whenever she wanted. Paradise.

She shook her head and started to rise, tugging on her hand.

"Lindsay, I can't let you go."

"You don't have the right to say that," she protested. She managed to get to her feet, but Gil stood also and pulled her against him. "Gil, we're right in the middle of town. Everyone will see—"

Apparently he didn't care, since his lips covered hers. Lindsay tried to resist his magic, but that was one thing she hadn't succeeded in accomplishing since her return. Her arms slid around his neck.

"You two are going to have to stop that!" Caleb roared, calling even more attention to the two of them. "Unless you've got something to tell me," he added, a grin on his face.

Lindsay jerked away from Gil. "No! No, there's nothing to tell."

"Yes, sir, you're right. We have something to tell you," Gil contradicted.

Lindsay stared at him in shock. What was he doing? Letting her father manipulate him?

"I want to marry your daughter," Gil continued, as if they were sitting down, chatting. "If she'll have me."

Lindsay stiffened. "Rafe is right. You are crazy!" Then she ran out of the coffee shop.

Gil wanted to chase after her. But he figured he needed to mend a few fences with her father, first.

"You serious?" Caleb asked.

"Oh, yeah. I tried to fight it, but I can't stay away from her. She—she completes me."

Caleb nodded, a smile on his face. "Yeah. Her mother does the same for me. Well, good. You'll get her out of the dress shop and back in a home, where she belongs."

Gil knew he'd prefer to have Lindsay at home, with her life centered around him. But he also wanted her to be happy—and to make her own decisions. He had learned a few lessons since Thanksgiving. Particularly the part about respecting her decisions, especially if her decision was to choose him. "No, sir. Lindsay will keep the store, if that's what she wants."

"Now, boy, you need to begin as you mean to go on, and a man has to be boss in his house," Caleb warned, not looking pleased.

"I intend to," Gil said with a smile. "Do we have your blessing?"

"Of course you do. I'm happy my daughter is going to marry a rancher. Best thing for her."

"I hope she will. She didn't say yes."

"She will," Caleb assured him.

Gil wished he was as confident.

"Gil must not be getting much work done on his ranch these days," Kelly teased as she saw the cowboy heading for their shop again. He'd been in every day for the past week. At first Lindsay had ignored him. Finally, on Wednesday, she'd gone for coffee again. And yesterday, too. He'd kept the conversation on easy topics. Kathy's pregnancy. The remodeling. Rafe's behavior.

Today, Gil strode into the shop at lunchtime. "Morning, ladies."

Kelly greeted him cheerfully. Lindsay frowned at him.

He leaned over and kissed her. A brief salute that had her heart racing.

"I thought I'd take you to lunch today and maybe out to the ranch to see the progress we've made on the house," he said.

"I can't do that!" she exclaimed, drawing away from him. "I can't leave Kelly alone. We have Andrew here. It takes two of us—"

"Actually," Kelly said, grinning, "Mom is coming in a few minutes to pick up Andrew and take him home with her. She's thinking about cutting back on her work hours and spending more time with her grandson."

"Then we could use the time with both of us here, to go over those latest bills. And to plan the trip to the Spring Market in Dallas."

"Later," Kelly said, easily dismissing Lindsay's suggestion.

Gil stood patiently waiting.

Lindsay looked at her friend and then Gil. Suddenly she said, "You're conspiring against me!"

Kelly stepped over and hugged her. "We're trying to get you to relax, have a little fun. You've been a major workaholic since we got the loan."

Lindsay felt a little hurt by Kelly's words. "Fine. I'll take the rest of the day off. But that doesn't mean I'm going to your place!" she snapped at Gil.

Gil shrugged his shoulders, as if her decision didn't matter, but he said, "Okay, but Rafe will be real disappointed. He made lunch for you."

"Gil Daniels, you're trying to blackmail me!"

"Yeah. Is it working?" he asked with his biggest smile.

Lindsay wanted to give in so badly. She was dying to see how the house was coming along. She'd asked a few casual questions of Jason, but she couldn't ask too much or he'd get suspicious.

She enjoyed Rafe and she'd like to see him again.

Most of all, she wanted to be in Gil's arms. But there was a price to pay for that luxury. Her father had mentioned something last night about her being in her rightful place, a man's kitchen, when, not if, she married Gil.

"I am not giving up my shop."

Her words seemed to surprise Gil and Kelly.

"Of course not," Kelly said hurriedly.

"Why would you?" Gil asked.

"My father said—he insinuated that I should marry you and stay home barefoot and pregnant!"

Gil grinned. "I don't have a problem with either of those conditions," he said, his gaze drifting to her feet, "but only if that's what you want. I'll admit I'd kind of miss the professional Miss Crawford in her business suits, in that case."

"You would?" she asked, suspicious in spite of the thrill that ran through her.

"Oh, yeah. Killer legs like yours are too good to be covered up."

"But I work in fashion," she pointed out.

"Yeah. And I think you're going to be a big success. I heard two ladies talking yesterday, claiming your shop was the only place in Lawton to get great clothes."

Kelly and Lindsay exchanged exultant looks.

"We're just getting started," Lindsay said, warning in her voice.

"I figured."

Lindsay stared at him, unsure what to think. He'd

been so adamant against any involvement in fashion, she hadn't thought he could ever accept what she did for a living.

"Sweetheart, Rafe explained it to me."

"Rafe? You discussed our—you talked with Rafe?"

"Hell, no! He talked, I listened. He said the only real question was whether I trusted you to stay." He put his hands on her shoulders. "I watched you come back to your family, even though they didn't treat you right, and fight for a relationship with them. I've watched you and Kelly join together, renewing your friendship. Why wouldn't I trust you to stay…if you loved me?"

She fought the urge to fall into his arms. "We haven't known each other very long."

"No, we haven't, though I realized I was in trouble when I woke up in that motel with you in my arms." He grinned when Kelly gasped. "Her father's reaction was a little more volatile."

"I can imagine," Kelly said with a laugh. "Um, maybe I'd better dust the front windows." She moved away to give them some privacy.

"Gil, I don't—"

He kissed her. "Don't think, sweetheart. When I think, I let all kinds of silly reasons come between us. But we're right together." He kissed her again. "I'll wait as long as it takes for you to agree. But come with me today, so I can show you what your new home is going to look like."

"And you wouldn't insist I leave the store? You wouldn't get upset if I wore silk or lace or—"

"As long as I get to take it off of you, you can

wear whatever you like,'' he assured her, his lips
returning to hers.

Lindsay slid her arms around his neck and opened
to him, delighted to have found the home she'd
longed for, where she could be herself and so much
more. She'd become her own woman. Now she could
be Gil's woman, too.

Epilogue

"There you go again, always kissing her!" Caleb complained as he entered the kitchen. "Can't you two find somewhere private?"

"Well, my bedroom's not crowded," Lindsay suggested with a grin, knowing what her father's reaction would be.

"No!" Caleb roared. "You're getting married in two days. I think you can wait that long." He grabbed the pitcher of tea and hurried out of the room.

"I think your dad is going to be glad when we're married," Gil murmured, nuzzling her neck, his arms still holding her close.

"I don't think he's the only one," she said with a hopeful smile. Gil's response was all she could've wanted. But since they'd promised to wait before they headed for a bedroom, she finally drew back. "I can't wait either."

"Yeah," Gil said, his gaze fixed on her lips, his voice husky.

"I'm glad you and Brad are getting along so well."

He rolled his eyes. "He's fine. I just hadn't spent any time with him."

"He's fitting in well here. And I'm glad Rafe came, too. He's okay about staying in the house with us, isn't he? You convinced him?" Rafe had offered to move out as soon as they married, but both she and Gil had protested. Gil had changed his plans with Jason Powell, making Rafe a self-contained apartment on the ground floor, so he'd have some privacy. And they would, too.

"Yeah, everything is going just the way it should."

"Or it will be in two more days," she added.

"Yeah. Christmas Eve. You just wanted to get more presents, that's why you agreed to that date for the wedding," he teased.

"It made sense. Abby and Logan would be here, with their baby. Kathy and Brad were already coming. I wanted all the family around us."

"Yeah, and it meant we didn't have to wait too long," Gil added, grinning. "'Cause I should tell you, lady, once I get you in my bed, I may not let you out of it for at least a month."

"A week is all you get, cowboy, before I have to be back at the store. But every night, I'm all yours, for as long as you want."

"I can't ask for anything more, sweetheart," he assured her as his lips covered hers once more.

* * * * *